Christmas is ...
and get ready for tw...
that will ...

MISTLETO...

Christmas Kisses, Yuletide Vows

After the death of their parents, cousins Penny and
Sally must face Christmas alone. But the girls are
determined to keep their family alive in their hearts
and pull together. So each prepares for Christmas,
but a surprise awaits them both…

The Cowboy's Christmas Proposal

Penny Bradford has no idea how to run her family
ranch, so she hires rugged rancher Jake Larson to
help. Penny knows that Jake can be trusted with the
ranch…but what about her heart?

Next month…

Snowbound with Mr Right

Sally Rogers loves the small town of Bailey,
and her store is the heart and soul of the community.
So when city-slicker Hunter Bedford arrives and
offers to buy her out, Sally is furious. The store is
all she has left of her family and she'll never sell.
But with the winter weather approaching, Sally finds
herself trapped with Hunter—and, what's more,
she's beginning to like it…

*Don't miss this heart-warming duet about family
and love, especially for the festive season, brought to
you by bestselling author Judy Christenberry!*

THE COWBOY'S CHRISTMAS PROPOSAL

BY
JUDY CHRISTENBERRY

™MILLS & BOON®

Pure reading pleasure

First published in Great Britain 2007
Harlequin Mills & Boon Limited,
Eton House, 18-24 Paradise Road, Richmond, Surrey TW9 1SR

© Judy Russell Christenberry 2007

ISBN: 978 0 263 85465 7

Set in Times Roman 13 on 15½ pt
02-1107-44327

Printed and bound in Spain
by Litografia Rosés, S.A., Barcelona

Judy Christenberry has been writing romances for fifteen years, because she loves happy endings as much as her readers do. A former French teacher, Judy now devotes herself to writing full-time. She hopes readers have as much fun reading her stories as she does writing them. She spends her spare time reading, watching her favourite sports teams, and keeping track of her two daughters. Judy's a native Texan and lives in Dallas.

PROLOGUE

Two attractive young ladies held hands as they stood by the four graves, tears streaking their cheeks as they struggled to overcome their emotions.

"At least we know they didn't suffer," one of the girls said, sniffing away her tears, the morning sun glinting off her shiny blond hair.

"No," the brunette agreed, "but they were much too young to die so soon."

"I know." She gulped back her emotions. "It means we're our only family now, you and I. We're going to have to stick together if we're going to continue."

"Yes. And that's what they would've wanted, for us to continue."

They were interrupted by the townspeople in Bailey, Colorado, wanting to express their condolences. The young cousins stood shoulder to shoulder and greeted their neighbors and friends. The deaths of their parents in a car accident, having traveled to Denver for a football game and run head-on with an eighteen-wheeler on the way home, had been totally unexpected and the tragic loss had taken everyone by surprise.

"You girls should ask for help when you need it. You're awfully young to be on your own," one neighbor had told them. They exchanged looks but received the piece of advice graciously. They were both twenty-five, a reasonable age to be independent, but neither had wanted it to be like this.

They received many offers of help, but they didn't expect to ask for any. They both thought they had a plan laid out to carry on their lives and their beloved family traditions.

But then they hadn't planned to be alone, either.

CHAPTER ONE

PENNY BRADFORD strode toward the bunk-house, knowing she was getting there late, but she needed to talk to Gerald Butler, her ranch manager.

She was grateful she had her father's trusted manager to rely on. Because of her brother's unexpected death at the age of sixteen, she hadn't been taught much of anything about ranching. Grieved by his death, her father had feared she might die also and had decided that Penny would instead be sheltered from ranch work and showered with affection. She had become her father's princess and his tragic death in a car wreck with her mother had devastated her.

But now it was time for Penny to start learning about running a ranch and Gerald had agreed to teach her. She had planned to meet him later that morning, but something else had come up and she had gone in search of him earlier than anticipated. She reached the bunkhouse and stood for a moment to draw a deep breath and prepare to knock on the door. Before she could do that, there was an uproar of laughter.

Leaning forward, she listened to determine what could be so funny and froze upon hearing her manager's betrayal.

"I don't see why I shouldn't continue. If I could fool her dad, the girl ought to be ridiculously easy. She'll never have any idea that I'm skimming off the top. Why, I've collected more than fifty thousand a year for the past four years."

Penny backed away from the bunkhouse in shock. When she thought she couldn't be heard, she turned and ran back to the ranch house.

Inside the house, she reached for the phone and called her cousin. "Oh, Sally, thank goodness. I—I just heard Gerald bragging that he's been skimming at least fifty thousand a year off Dad for the past four years! What do I do?"

"Oh, my! Penny, that's awful. Well, there's really only one thing you can do—you'll have to fire him. Clearly the man isn't to be trusted so you make sure he leaves with nothing that belongs to the ranch. Will you be able to do that?"

Penny took a deep breath. "Yes, I can do that I'm so angry that he would treat my father that way. The only problem is, what do I do then? You know I know nothing about ranching. Dad refused to teach me, afraid I might have an accident, and Gerald is the only one who knows how the ranch works."

"I know, you are going to need some help. Wasn't your dad friends with Dexter Williams? He's the biggest rancher in the area, maybe he could recommend someone trustworthy to replace Gerald."

"Good idea. Thank you. I couldn't think for a moment. I think I'll get the sheriff to escort Gerald off the ranch. I'll go see him first thing in the morning and let him come back out with me. I doubt I could prove what Gerald has done, but I should be able to scare him enough to send him on his way."

"I'm glad I could help. Let me know what happens."

"I will, Thanks, Sally, I'll call you tomorrow." Penny hung up the phone and prepared to take her first difficult step as ranch owner.

"Mr. Williams, I appreciate your taking the time to talk to me. I know you and Dad were friends, and I need your advice."

"Of course, Penny. How can I help you?"

"I need a ranch manager, someone known for his honesty as well as his ranching skills, and who would be willing to teach me about ranching."

"Hmm, that's a tall order, my dear. What happened to Gerald?"

"I fired him this morning after I discovered he was ripping Dad off. Now I need a replacement"

"I'm sorry to hear that, Penny, your father was a good man. Decent honest ranch managers are hard to find." Suddenly, as if a lightbulb went off in his head, he said, "But I may know just the man for you. He's ready for a managerial job but there isn't an opening here for him."

"What's his name?"

"Jake Larson. There's only one thing about

him." The old man began to chuckle as he decided how to phrase his next words. "He has a bit of a reputation…as a ladies' man, so you'd best keep your distance."

"Oh, I'm sure I can do that, Mr Williams, as long as he can be trusted on my ranch."

"Oh, he's completely trustworthy. I'll send him over to talk to you first thing in the morning."

"Thank you, Mr. Williams. I appreciate your assistance."

"I'm glad to help out, Penny. Now you let me know if there is anything else I can do for you."

Penny replaced the receiver, pleased that she had found an answer to her problem, but curious as to exactly what kind of man Jake Larson was.

Jake Larson walked up to the big house, gritting his teeth. He hoped it was Dexter who wanted to see him and not the much younger Mrs. Williams. She'd been chasing Jake all summer and he'd been expecting to be fired.

It wouldn't be fair, because he had no interest in the woman, but he couldn't convince her of that. He had even less of a chance to convince Dexter it was his wife who was doing the chasing.

So he'd take what was coming as well as he could.

He knocked on the back door and waited. Dexter appeared and opened the door to him. "Come on in, Jake."

"Yes, sir."

"Let's go to my office and have a chat."

Jake figured he'd be lucky if Dexter gave him a recommendation.

Once they were seated, Dexter said, "Jake, we both know things can't continue as they have been. I didn't want to let you go, because you're a good man. That wouldn't be fair. So I've found you another job."

Jake's head came up and he stared at his boss. "I usually find my own jobs."

"Okay, I'll be honest with you. You'll be doing me a favor if you take this job. You're ready for it. The daughter of a friend of mine who recently died needs a new manager. Someone who can run the ranch and also teach her about ranching."

Jake frowned. He'd been wanting a managerial job. That was great news. Teaching a woman about ranching didn't appeal.

"I'm not sure I'm right for the job."

"You're right for it, Jake. And we both know you can't stay here."

"Yeah, I know, but—what ranch?"

"The Rocking B ranch, on the other side of town. It's a good operation, but she's just found out her manager has been skimming the profits for the past four years."

"That's the one with the brand that looks like a hat?"

"Yeah, that's them."

"I guess I could talk to her."

"Good. She's expecting you this morning. Pack your things. I'll let my wife know you've moved on."

"Yes, sir." Jake figured he'd talk to the lady about the job. Then, if he didn't like the situation, he'd move on. He'd saved some money and would be all right for a few months.

When he got back to the bunkhouse, the men had already gone out on their assignments. He'd call a couple of them after he got settled. They all knew the situation, so they wouldn't be surprised to find him gone.

It didn't take long to pack up his belongings. The main thing he would take with him was his mount. He and Apache had been partners for the past four years. He was well trained and Jake had had a lot of offers for Apache, but he knew the value of his horse.

His truck and trailer had been well-maintained and would come in useful wherever he worked. He loaded Apache in the trailer and connected it to his truck, then he threw his belongings into the back seat and took the hourlong drive to the Rocking B ranch.

Penny paced the kitchen, waiting for Jake Larson to show up for his new job. She hoped Dexter Williams had explained everything. She thought he should be there at any time.

It would be a relief to have someone in charge of the ranch. She knew so little about the decisions she should make. She intended to study hard to learn what she should do, but she would have to have some help.

She heard a vehicle turn in her long driveway. She peeked out the window and saw a truck and trailer come to a halt. Holding her breath, she waited until the truck door opened and a tall, rangy man got out. Dexter had told her he was a ladies' man, and she intended to make her lack of interest very clear.

When he came closer, she was surprised to see he wasn't what one would call a "pretty boy." He had rugged good looks that might tempt many women, but not her. She needed to learn ranching, not find a boyfriend.

The man strode toward the back door. She waited until he knocked and taking a deep breath, she opened the door. "Yes?"

"I'm Jake Larson. Mr. Williams suggested I come talk to you about a job you have open."

"Yes, come in, Mr. Larson." She moved back to give him room. Then she walked toward the cabinet. "Coffee?" she asked.

"Yes, please."

Okay, so he had nice manners. She poured him a mug of coffee and one for herself. Then she offered him a seat at the table. She sat down across from him. "I hope Mr. Williams explained that you'd also be doing some teaching. I don't know much about ranching."

"Yes, ma'am, he mentioned that. I'm not sure I'm the one for the job. I'm not used to explaining the hows and whys of my job."

"I can understand that, Mr. Larson, but I'm afraid that aspect of the job is absolutely necessary."

"If you trust me to do the job, why do I need to teach you?"

"Because I believe I need to know the job as well as you. Otherwise, I can't give my opinion."

"It's not something easy to learn. You realize I can't teach you what I know in six months or a year. It takes longer than that."

"I understand. But I have to start somewhere."

"Do you understand that you may have to postpone asking questions until the end of the day? There isn't always enough time to do that during the day."

"Yes, I can be flexible."

He stared at her for several minutes, and she held her breath. His dark brown eyes were hard to read. She had no idea if he'd accept the job or turn her down.

Finally he extended his hand across the table. "Very well, Miss Bradford, if you want me, I'll take the job."

She shook his hand, liking the strength of that hand as it grasped hers. "Yes, I'd like that. May I show you your quarters?"

"Yes, ma'am."

She got up and led the way out of the kitchen

to the bunkhouse. She had cleaned out a private room at the end of the building yesterday after her talk with Dexter Williams.

"This is the manager's room. I hope it will be satisfactory for you, but let me know if there's anything else you need. You can put your dirty laundry in this basket. I'm hiring a housekeeper and I'll instruct her to do your laundry once a week." Penny paused and looked at the ground before continuing. "I didn't fire any of the other cowboys, but if you catch any of them cheating, feel free to fire them."

"Yes, ma'am."

"Will your quarters be satisfactory?"

"Yes, ma'am."

"Then I'll leave you. The men should be in before sunset. One of the men will come in early. He's the designated cook."

He nodded his head.

Penny returned his nod and got out of there before she started answering yes sir in response to his yes ma'ams. She strode across the grass that parted the main house from the bunkhouse. Hopefully Mr. Larson would do his job well and teach her about ranching for many years to come.

* * *

Jake watched her walk back to the house. She seemed awfully young to him. Maybe it was her name. It made him think of a child. Not that she looked like a little girl. Her body was definitely that of a woman.

But he didn't intend to show any interest in her. He'd learned his lesson. Romance and ranching didn't work for him. He intended to avoid any hint of flirtation.

Looking around the room, he decided he liked having a separate room from the rest of the men. He'd tired of sharing large rooms with everyone else. If the cook was good, he'd be happy. Good food made the difference in some jobs.

Before he settled in his room, he went out and unloaded Apache and put him in a corral. "You'll be okay here, Apache. I'll be back in the morning." He checked the water barrel before he went back in and stored things away, making himself at home. Having his laundry done was handy, too. And he had a desk for doing paperwork.

Dexter had been right. He was ready for this job. And he'd even teach the woman about ranching. After all, it was a job he loved.

* * *

Penny ate some lunch and then began pacing the floor again. She had someone coming to interview for the housekeeper's job and she was feeling anxious. Penny had always helped her mother in the house, but if she was going to be on horseback most of the day learning ranching, she wouldn't be able to keep the house in order or prepare good meals. A housekeeper was a necessity.

But she wasn't sure she could stand to have a stranger live with her, in the same house. She'd always shared the house with her parents and brother, but no one else. Penny was more nervous about this interview than she had been with Jake Larson.

Another vehicle pulled into the driveway. Penny watched through the window at the lady who got out. She guessed her age was about fifty, a little overweight, but not much. Even better, she had a pleasant expression on her face.

Again, Penny waited until her visitor knocked and then opened the door. The lady introduced herself as Harriet Buckner. Penny invited her in.

"My, what a lovely kitchen," the woman said, looking around.

"Yes, my father had it redone last year for my—my mother."

"Oh, yes, I heard. I'm so sorry for your loss."

"Thank you. I helped my mother with the housework and cooking, but now I'm going to be riding out each day with my new manager to learn the business and I don't think I'll feel like cooking and cleaning also." She drew a deep breath. "So, I'm looking for a house-keeper who can do all those things herself."

The woman nodded. "I've been cooking since I was a little girl and I enjoy it. And I'm good at cleaning. Are there any duties you're especially looking for?"

"No, I don't think so. But I did tell the new manager you'd do his laundry. I put a laundry basket in his room. And maybe occasional baking for the men. They seldom have time for any cooking that takes time."

"Of course. So it'll just be you and me for meals here in the house?"

"Yes, unless I invite someone. My cousin and I try to visit as much as we can. Or I might ask the manager to join us occasionally so I can ask questions about something that happened. I'm a raw beginner at ranching."

"I see. I could always prepare enough food for three. Then I'd eat the leftovers the next day for lunch, so it wouldn't go to waste."

"Yes, that would work. Do you think you'd like the job?"

"It sounds perfect to me."

Penny drew a deep breath. "I'll show you your room." She'd already decided the guest room on the first floor would be perfect for the housekeeper. She led her down the hall and opened the door. "This bedroom would be yours and it has an attached bathroom for you."

"Oh, my, it's quite lovely. I'll be very comfortable here."

"All right. Do you need to go back to Trinity to get your belongings before you move in?" To Penny's surprise, the woman's face turned a bright red.

"No! I—I took my belongings with me. You see, the rancher I worked for previously decided he—he was interested in marrying me, but it had only been a month since his wife had died. I thought he was looking for a way to have my services without paying me a salary. I wasn't interested."

"Oh, yes, I understand. That would be awkward."

"Yes. I really appreciate you giving me this job. I promise I'll do my best. You just let me know what you want me to do."

"I will. I'll take care of my own bedroom. You'll just need to clean the downstairs."

"You're making the job sound too easy."

"No, I'm sure you'll be busy."

"Okay. What time do you want breakfast on the table?"

"Oh! I didn't ask my new manager what time he wanted me to be ready. I'll go ask him while you're getting settled."

Penny stepped out on the back porch and gave a sigh of relief. Harriet seemed like she'd be okay and easy to get along with.

She walked down to the bunkhouse and knocked on the door. When there was no answer, she stepped inside and moved to the manager's room. No answer there, either.

Moving back outside, she noted that the truck and trailer had been parked out of the way but were still there. She moved to the main barn that held some of the hay supply but also housed any cows that had problems with their calves, or injured horses.

No one there.

Then she heard that deep voice that fascinated her. It was coming from the nearest corral. She moved out into the cold air again and found him petting a horse.

"Beautiful horse. Is he yours?" she asked.

Jake spun around as if she'd crept up behind him. "Uh, yeah, he's mine. His name is Apache. I—I took a little hay to feed him."

"That's fine. The men usually put their rides in a corral in winter. It makes it much easier to get started in the morning and more efficient to feed them when they are in a corral."

"Yeah, I figured."

"I needed to ask you what time you wanted to start in the morning."

"I usually eat breakfast at six-thirty. There's barely enough light at seven in the winter. That's when you'd need to be in the saddle. Have you ever ridden a horse before?"

"Yes, I'm a proficient rider. It's the one thing my dad insisted I learn."

"Okay, then I'll see you at seven."

"Do we take our lunches with us?"

"Would you like us to have a picnic to-gether?" he asked, sarcasm in his voice.

Penny stiffened. "No, I didn't mean to have a picnic, but I'm used to eating lunch. I didn't want to waste time coming in for lunch."

"You go ahead and bring along what you need to eat, but it has to be eaten while you're in the saddle. I don't eat lunch."

"Fine. I'll see you at seven in the morning."

She didn't wait for an answer. Spinning on her heels she headed for the house.

CHAPTER TWO

PENNY marched back to the house, her teeth clenched. The nerve of the man! He thought she was hoping for a romantic picnic? He had the wrong idea about her. She would have to be on her toes to make sure he didn't get that idea again!

When she reached the house, she went to Harriet's bedroom. The lady was storing away her clothes.

"Is everything okay, Harriet?"

"Yes, ma'am. What time did the manager expect you to be ready?"

"He said seven. His name is Jake Larson, by the way, but don't expect him to be friendly."

"Oh? And you hired him anyway?"

"I was warned that though he's honest, he has problems with thinking he's a ladies' man. When I asked him if I should bring a lunch tomorrow, he thought I was expecting a romantic picnic!"

"And that's what he wanted?"

Penny looked at Harriet, frowning. "No," she said slowly, "his question was sarcastic, as if that was the last thing he wanted."

Harriet didn't say anything.

"Maybe he's changed his tune, but I'll be on my toes anyway. I'm not looking for a boyfriend."

"So you're not taking a lunch?"

"I need something to eat that I can manage in the saddle. Do you know what I can take with me?"

"A sandwich will work. It won't spoil in winter. An apple works okay, too, and what you don't eat can be fed to your horse."

"Good idea. Oh, rats. I didn't think about bringing my horse to the corral. I'll be back in a little while. You might want to check the supplies in the kitchen when you have time."

"Right. I'll do that."

Penny hurried out of the house after pulling on her coat and adding a wool cap and gloves. She walked to the barn, collected a bridle and opened the gate that led to the pasture where the active horses were kept. She saw the horse she preferred to ride, a dark colored mare named Stormy that her father had given her when she'd first learned to ride.

It took a few minutes to reach Stormy and talk her into accepting the bridle. Then Penny led her to the corral where Apache was waiting. She got some hay for Stormy and settled her down in the corral. Then she removed the bridle and, after patting Stormy's neck, replaced her bridle in the tack room and headed back to the house.

When she entered the house, she could smell fresh coffee. In the kitchen, she found Harriet going through the pantry.

"I'm going to have some of that coffee, if you don't mind."

"Of course not." Harriet stepped out of the pantry. "You've got just about everything I can foresee for the immediate future. Your freezer is well stocked, too."

"Good. I've got my horse penned up ready for tomorrow. I'll need coffee in the morning and oatmeal with bacon and toast or eggs with bacon and toast. Either one, or you can rotate them. I like pancakes on Saturday morning and even Sunday morning when I can eat more leisurely."

"That sounds good to me. Though I might

suggest cinnamon rolls one of those mornings. I make them from scratch, and they're quite good, if I do say so myself."

"Mmm, I agree. They sound perfect for a cold morning."

"Good. I'll cook a couple of steaks for dinner because I can thaw them quickly, if that's okay. And do you like salads?"

"Yes, I do. I'm willing to try most anything."

"Then we'll get along fine."

"Thank you, Harriet. I'm glad things are working out well for one of my new employees!"

It was quite cold the next morning when Penny stepped outside. She had a wool cap on her head under the cowboy hat her dad had always worn. Leather gloves with wool lining were on her hands, and her jacket was snapped closed to her throat over a wool sweater.

She carried a package that held her lunch. She wasn't going to try to be tough just to impress Jake Larson. She knew the day would be hard on her as it was. She was a good horsewoman, but she seldom rode more than three or four hours.

A canteen was strapped over her shoulder

and would be added to her saddle. Also over her shoulder was a plastic raincoat her dad had always taken with him.

She had her dad on her mind today. He'd never expected her to be in this situation and never prepared her for the job. She had always been his little girl and no matter how many times she had asked, her father had always discouraged her from learning the ropes. Certainly learning about ranching now was important to Penny, especially if she was going to make a success of the ranch, but more important now was proving herself to her father, even though he wasn't there.

When she reached the corral, after getting her bridle and saddle and saddle blanket, she found Stormy and got her ready for the day ahead. She added the raincoat, carefully tied it down so it wouldn't startle the horse and placed her canteen in one side of the saddlebags. The other side held her lunch.

Swinging into the saddle just at seven o'clock, she was ready to go, she hoped, as the men came out to mount up. Jake was talking to several of the men and looked up in surprise when the others greeted her as Penny.

She spoke to the men, but she remained silent as Jake approached her. Nervous, she licked her lips and waited for his response.

"I thought I'd meet you up at the house."

"I assumed it'd be quicker to meet you here, ready to go." She kept her voice crisp.

"Very well. I'll be saddled in just a minute."

He efficiently prepared his horse and swung into the saddle. She moved ahead of him and opened the corral gate. He followed her out into the pasture.

"I thought we might ride over the property to make sure I know the perimeters this morning. Are you up for that?" he asked Penny.

"Of course."

"Do you know the perimeters?"

"Yes, I do." She led the way and gave a good description of each pasture. She'd listened avidly to her father's talk at the dinner table. They came across several of the other cowboys already at work. Jake told her he'd talked to the men about the assignments they had been given before the past manager had left. "I told them to continue with what they were already doing until I figured out what I wanted to change."

"Did they all agree with that?"

"Yes, they did. If they hadn't, I would've fired them on the spot."

"I see." She didn't really have an argument against such behavior, but she didn't want to say so.

She was able to answer most questions he asked, though he didn't ask many.

Around noon, Penny took her lunch out of her saddlebag and quietly ate as she rode. She was feeling the strain of five hours in the saddle, but she didn't intend to ask for a break.

Fortunately, after she finished her lunch, Jake suggested they stop. They dismounted by a mountain stream that ran through the property. Jake told her to stretch her legs after she had returned to her mount, they both walked in the direction of a nearby stream. She took both horses to the water and let them drink. Then she took her apple core and broke it in half, feeding each horse its share.

Jake gave her a quick look when she returned. "What did you feed the horses?"

"They each got half of my apple core," she told him, a challenge in her voice.

"Okay. Thanks for sharing with Apache. He's particularly fond of apples."

"So is Stormy."

"Ah. I wondered about her name."

As much as she dreaded mounting again, she turned to do so.

"Mind if we walk a little ways along this stream? I'd like to see how full it is."

"All right." She took Stormy's reins and walked along the stream, grateful for the chance to stretch her legs.

Much to her surprise, Jake began talking about the use of this particular pasture, noting what he'd read in a ranching journal about the treatment in vogue among ranchers. She asked several questions, hesitant at first.

Jake answered each of her questions calmly, not changing his manner if the question was good or bad. Then he asked some questions about her dad and how he had handled certain things. Some questions Penny couldn't answer, but she suddenly realized she might have the answers at home.

"I'd forgotten about it until now, but Dad kept a journal in which he recorded what he did each year. Then he could look back from one year to another. Would you like to take a look at it?"

"I'd like that very much if you don't mind. I promise I'll return it in the same shape it is now. I assume you value things like that."

"Yes, thank you, I do. I haven't had much time—I haven't gone through their things yet."

"It can wait if you're not ready," he said gruffly.

"No, I can—I'll look for it tonight."

"I appreciate it. I assume your dad's ranch was profitable?"

"Yes, but I hadn't realized how much until I overheard my previous manager brag about collecting fifty thousand dollars each year without my father even realizing it."

Jake whistled. "That's a hefty sum not to be missed."

"I know. I can only assume that my dad trusted him completely."

"I'm sorry to hear that. One of the things I'll teach you is how to recognize things like that. I did a lot of the paperwork for Dexter—I mean, Mr. Williams, so I can show you how to check over your accounts."

"Good. I'll look forward to that."

"Okay, I think we should mount up and get under way. I'd like to get back to the barn by dark."

The walk had helped Penny's legs. She didn't know if the break had been for her benefit or not, but she had appreciated it.

However, five hours later, when they'd still only covered half the ranch, she barely managed to hold on to the saddle horn as they'd reached the barn. The men were already in the bunkhouse, so she didn't have to worry about an audience other than Jake. She slid out of the saddle hoping she could hold on long enough for her legs to bear her.

Much to her surprise, Jake said from right behind her, "You can go ahead to the house. I'll unsaddle your horse."

"No! I—I'll do it."

"Penny, you did well today, but I know you're not used to riding for so many hours. After you get used to it, you can unsaddle Stormy, but today I'll do it."

She took a brief look at his eyes. They were warm and brown and something in them told her to trust in Jake a little. The feeling made her nervous. Then she nodded. "Okay, thanks." She forced her fingers to release the saddle horn and almost fell, but strong hands caught her arms. A tingling sensation ran the length of Penny's spine and she knew that the day had tired her more than she thought.

"Are you okay?"

"Y-yes, thank you." She pulled away and stumbled to the gate and went through. Gradually the walking helped her legs unkink and she managed to get to the ranch house.

When she opened the back door, she was almost knocked off her feet by a wave of warm air that smelled so good. She made it to the breakfast table and fell into a chair.

"Long day?" Harriet asked, sympathy in her voice as she sat a full mug of coffee in front of her.

Penny didn't answer until she'd had her first sip of coffee. "Oh, my, that tastes good, Harriet. Yes, it was a long day. And we only covered half the ranch. We'll finish the tour tomorrow."

"Maybe it will get a little easier as you go along," Harriet said. "Do you want dinner now, or do you want a hot shower first?"

"Mmm, do you mind? I think I might enjoy the food more after a hot shower."

"Of course I don't mind. It'll be ready when you are."

"Thanks, Harriet." She stood and left the room, taking her coffee with her.

Half an hour later, she sat down at the table for a delicious meal. She and Harriet chatted a little, but Penny was too tired to talk about much. However, when dinner was through, Harriet suggested she go to bed at once.

"I can't. I promised Jake I'd find Dad's journal. He'd like to see what Dad was doing with the pastures."

"Can I help you look?" Harriet asked.

Penny took a deep breath. "Would you mind? It shouldn't be that difficult to find, but—but I haven't been in their room since—since they died. It might help having someone else with me."

"Of course I don't mind. Let me rinse the dishes while you rest. Then we'll go up together."

Penny sat there finishing her coffee, fighting the guilty feelings as she watched Harriet work. "I feel bad leaving all the work to you, Harriet."

"Nonsense, child. That's why I'm here. Believe me, if I'd ridden a horse all day, I wouldn't be able to walk."

A few minutes later, the pair went up the

stairs together. Penny felt her feet dragging and blamed it on her day's activities. But she could feel the emotion building in her throat.

Her parents had been dead now for a number of months. It hadn't been until recently that she'd thought about cleaning out their room, but she just hadn't had the courage to go through with it. It had been impossible to face erasing all memory of her parents.

"Do you want a few minutes alone or do you want me to go in with you?" Harriet asked.

"No, I—I don't want to go in alone."

Harriet opened the door and walked through, letting Penny take her time.

"My, your mother was a good housekeeper."

"Yes, she didn't like to leave a mess behind." Penny looked at the room that hadn't changed since she was a child. The lavender print on the bedspread had faded with the years, but it still looked good.

"Do you have any idea where the journal would be?" Harriet asked gently.

"I think it'll be in his bedside stand. Mom always complained about him writing in it when she was trying to go to sleep."

Penny moved to the right side of the bed and

opened the drawer. There it was. He bought the same brand every year. She took it out of the drawer, letting her fingers rest on the binding for a moment. Slowly she opened the book, looking for his last entry. Then she found the book that preceded that one, in case Jake wanted to go back any further.

"Is this room much bigger than yours?" Harriet asked.

"Yes, it is," Penny answered in surprise.

"I could clean the room out for you, if you want to move in here."

"Oh, no! I—I couldn't do that."

"It's up to you, Penny, but your parents aren't going to be able to enjoy the room anymore—it's your home now."

"I know, you're right, but it still feels too soon—maybe in a week or two."

"You just let me know, but the clothes could be put to good use, the ones you don't want to keep. It gets cold up here in winter."

"That's true. I'll come up tomorrow night and take out any clothes I want to save. Then you can clean out their closet for me. If you have time."

"I'll have time."

"Thank you, Harriet."

Penny donned her coat and wool cap and gloves and went back outside in the cold night air.

She knocked on the door of the bunkhouse. There was the sound of scrambling as men grabbed for clothes. She waited patiently. When the door opened, she recognized one of the men, Barney. "Would you tell Mr. Larson that I need to see him?"

"Yes, ma'am, Penny. Just a minute."

Leaning against the wall of the building, she waited for the door to open again. When it finally did, Jake stepped outside. "Yes, ma'am?"

"I have my dad's journals for this year and last. Take your time with them."

Jake took the leather bound books and held them in his big hands. He turned the books over gently as though he knew their value and a sudden pain struck in Penny's chest. "Thank you, Penny. I appreciate you loaning these to me."

"Yes, well, good night Jake." She didn't wait for him to respond. She spun around and headed back to the house. In the distance she finally heard him say good-night.

Jake had learned several things about his new employer over the last day. One thing she wasn't a flirt, and further she didn't complain when the going got tough. Both of those won high marks in his book.

He'd worried about her asking for a lunch break, thinking she would complain about the hard day they faced. But it turned out he'd been wrong. She hadn't made her eating any big production. In fact, she'd almost acted as if she were ashamed that she needed to eat. And although she clearly wasn't used to riding such long hours, she'd never complained.

Now she'd delivered her father's journals, trusting them into his care. They would help him a lot in understanding the workings of the ranch. He already had a lot of questions and he didn't think she could answer all of them.

He took the books back inside.

"She assign you some homework, boss?"

"Yeah, she did. It appears her dad kept a journal about the place. I thought it could bring me up to speed quickly."

Several of the cowboys sat up, staring at him.

"Journals? You mean he kept notes about everything?"

"Yeah. I take it you didn't know?"

"Uh-no. You think he wrote things about us in there?"

"I don't know. But I'll let you know after I read them."

"Oh, yeah, sure, you do that, boss."

Jake went into his room and closed the door. It shut out the television the cowboys seemed to enjoy after a day's work. He wanted peace and quiet for what he was about to read. After only half an hour, he had already found the journals immensely helpful. The man hadn't wasted ink on poetry and the information he'd written had been detailed and to the point.

Settling back against his pillow, Jake turned back the pages and read to the day before the man died. Described there was just an ordinary day without a hint of the tragedy that was to follow. Penny's father had written about the cattle in the top pasture and how much he was expecting to make for them at a sale. He'd also documented his concerns regarding Gerald and a number of the other cowboys that still worked on the ranch. Jake knew that some of them would love to get their hands on the books now in his possession. He put the journals in a lock box he took with him wherever he lived. After he locked the lid, he slid the box under his bed, out of view. He'd read more tomorrow night, but he wanted to guarantee their safety until then.

He'd noticed the reaction of some of the men when he'd mentioned the existence of the journals. He hadn't taken a liking to one or two of the men right away. He might be wrong, but he'd thought those men might deserve a little extra attention.

There had been several comments in the book about some of them, but each time, Gerald assured the man he was wrong. Penny had been right—it seemed her father had trusted him implicitly.

Jake decided to tell Penny that her dad had been cleverly lied to by his manager, but that his instincts had been true. Maybe that would take away some of that pain he'd seen earlier in her blue eyes. He'd noticed how beautiful she was, but she was also young, and not to mention, his boss. He didn't intend to give in to any urges.

Jake thought back to Dexter Williams's wife. He hadn't had any urges for her, even though a lot of people had thought her beautiful. But her beauty had been paid for by her husband. After the death of his first wife, Dexter had fell headlong into marriage with a woman thirty years his junior. He had never realized that he couldn't trust her.

As far as Jake was concerned, he hoped Dexter's marriage worked out. Dexter obviously still believed that his wife was to be trusted and although Jake hadn't done anything to change that belief, Mrs. Williams had certainly tried.

Jake believed in honor, in a man or a woman. That was an attribute he looked for in everyone he met. It wasn't often easy to see, but time would always tell.

It was way too early to tell about Penny. Her beauty was evident, but he still couldn't be sure about her true character. What little he'd seen of her today had impressed him though and she was definitely from a good honest family. He was already forming a good opinion of her father's character, and he had never had the opportunity to meet the man. He looked forward to reading more tomorrow night.

Now he turned out the light and climbed into his bed. He settled down under the covers and closed his eyes.

* * *

Again the next morning, Penny was waiting for him when he reached the corral.

He hadn't slept well last night and was in a tetchy mood this morning. He looked at her, afraid his tiredness might be reflected on his face. "Are you wanting to start earlier than seven, ma'am?"

Penny stared at him, blinking her big blue eyes. "No, I just didn't want to be late."

"I can stand to wait a minute or two. Quit worrying about it."

"Okay. Are you okay, Mr. Larson?"

"I'm fine." Jake answered, angry at himself for losing his cool with her. She was his boss, even though she was only a young woman.

"Then let me know when you're ready."

"Did you bring your lunch with you today?"

"Yes. Did you want something?" Penny stared at him with her big blue eyes, determined not to be intimidated by him.

"I wouldn't turn down an apple if you've got an extra one."

"I'll ride up to the house and get an extra one."

He opened his mouth to protest, but she was already on her way. Maybe that was best. He'd get his horse saddled without her staring at him.

She was on her way back when he rode out of the corral to meet her. She handed over a big, red apple to him. "I'll let you carry it in your own saddlebag."

CHAPTER THREE

OKAY, so maybe he'd asked for her response. He swung down from his saddle and stowed the apple in his saddlebag. Then he mounted again. "Ready?"

"Yes," she said, not bothering to look his way.

He started out in the opposite direction of their ride yesterday. After a few minutes, when they were well away from the barn, he said, "I thought you might want to know that your father had doubts about several of the men riding for him."

"He did?" she asked, her eyes wide.

"Yeah, but every time he talked to Gerald about them, he told him he was wrong."

"And Gerald convinced him?"

"Not entirely, but your father didn't want to

go against Gerald without proof. He was keeping watch, intending to let them go as soon as he caught them red-handed in slacking off, or doing anything they shouldn't be doing. He hadn't come to the conclusion that Gerald was the main problem, but he was making his way there." After a moment of silence, he added, "I thought it might make you feel better to know that."

Penny was silent for a moment as she took in Jake's words. It had been kind of him to tell her about her father's concerns and it did make her feel better. When she spoke her voice was shaking slightly. "Thank you. Are you going to do anything about the ones he didn't trust?"

"Not unless I catch them red-handed, like your dad intended. They could change their ways. It certainly alarmed some of them that your dad had kept a journal."

"How could you tell?"

"By the fear on their faces when I told them."

"Then I doubt you'll be able to return the books, as you promised."

"Don't worry, I locked them in a box and hid it. It will be obvious if anyone tries looking for them."

She didn't look pleased with his security measures. "Let me know if they destroy them!"

"Penny, I'm sure no one will try."

She nudged her horse ahead of him, indicating she didn't want to chat about the journals any longer.

He let her lead for the next hour until he had some questions about the use of a pasture they were passing, but Penny didn't have the answer.

Jake didn't push her. He felt sure he'd find the answer in the journals. "Isn't it about time you ate your lunch?"

She looked up in surprise. "I suppose so. Is that a problem?"

"Not for me. I'm looking for an excuse to bite into that apple, but I didn't want to admit my weakness. But you don't seem in a hurry to eat today, even though it's after twelve."

"I didn't realize the time. It's flown by quickly."

"So are you ready to eat?"

"Yes, of course." She took out her lunch. "The sandwich I have is rather large. Would you like some of it?"

He looked at her, as if trying to determine her motive.

"I'm not trying to bribe you or gain some advantage. I'm just offering to share my sandwich."

He nodded. "Yeah, I'd like part of your sandwich if you're sure you can spare it."

She managed to separate about half her sandwich and hand it to him. He finished his share before she was half through.

"Thanks, that was good."

"I'll have Harriet make two sandwiches for tomorrow, if you'd like?"

"I don't want to cause any trouble."

"She won't mind. I don't think she has enough to do actually. When I left she was making pies for your dinner this evening."

"Pies? What kind?"

"Apple."

"I can't wait."

She studied him more closely. "You like sweets?"

"Sure. Doesn't everyone?"

"Yes, I guess so." He smiled a warm, genuine smile and Penny instantly reciprocated. The somber mood from before lifted between them. Penny was beginning to realize that there was a lot more to Jake Larson than just ranching.

"How are the meals in the bunkhouse?"

"Not bad. Cookie does a good job on regular stuff."

"Maybe Harriet's baking will make the meals better."

"So Harriet's working out fine for you?"

"Yes, she's a good cook. And she's willing to do whatever I need her to do. I'm feeling guilty because she does everything around the house."

He grinned. "You're putting in a full day, Penny. Let her do her job."

She glared at him. "I am."

They topped a hill and Jake discovered a source of water in the form of a pleasant lake. "Is this spring-fed?"

"Yes. Even in the middle of the summer, it's always ice cold."

"And does the water level change much?"

"No, not at all."

"Hmm. Your dad must've relied on this water supply a lot."

"Yes, I think so."

Jake swung down from his saddle and stuck a hand in the water. "You're right. It's certainly icy today."

"It is winter, Jake. Everything's cold."

"True. Want to dismount and eat our apples out of the wind?"

"I'd rather keep going so we get back before dark. Part of the perimeter is hard going."

"Have it your way," he said, swinging back up into the saddle. He reached back and took out the apple. "Okay, let's go."

They both ate in silence and continued on their journey. They stopped only to feed their horses the cores of their fruit and stretch their legs before carrying on. Jake didn't make an effort to linger. Penny had already made her feelings clear.

The afternoon ride wasn't easy, he'd admit. They seemed to climb mountains and then ride down them again. Jake didn't have to worry about conversation since they rode single file.

When they reached the barn, again just as daylight was fading, he told Penny that he wanted to spend the next day checking out what the cowboys were doing, but he'd rather she not mention that to any of them. He wanted his appearance to be a surprise.

"Fine," she replied and said nothing else until they reached the corral. No cowboys were in sight, but she simply said, "Tomorrow at seven?"

* * *

After taking care of her horse and putting away her tack, she left the barn area without even saying good-night.

Jake turned and stared at her retreating figure. Okay, so she was unhappy with him. So be it. They'd had a long day today, but she was the one who wanted to learn about ranching. He wasn't going to make it easy for her just because she was a woman.

He headed for the bunkhouse. Opening the door to his room, he knew at once someone had been in. It wasn't Harriet because his laundry was still in the basket. He slowly closed the door and found his lock box under his bed. Turning the lock, he opened the box and found both journals still in place. He took them out, relocked the box and replaced it under his bed.

Then he hid the journals inside his shirt, covered by his jacket, and went out into the main room. Once there, he noted several of the men watching him. He suspected those were the ones who had gone into his room.

He mentally noted the names and pasted on a smile. "I hear we have pie tonight boys."

"Aw, boss," Cookie complained, "I was keeping them pies a secret."

"Sorry, Cookie, I didn't know." He kept his gaze on the two men he suspected, noting they weren't swayed by the idea of pie. Suddenly, neither was he.

Penny dragged herself into the house that evening, feeling even worse than she had the day before.

Harriet took one look at her and poured her a cup of coffee. "Shower or dinner first?"

"I think I'll just wash up in the bathroom down here. I'm not sure I could even climb the stairs."

"I should mention that your cousin, Sally is coming to dinner. She called for you earlier and she seemed a little down so I invited her. I didn't think you'd mind."

Penny jumped to her feet and then groaned as her aching body protested. "Oh, Harriet, thank you, it'll be so good to see her. I'll go take a shower. Do you need any help?"

"No, honey, I'm fine. I'll have the table set before you get back down here."

Penny wasn't as fast as she'd intended. The

hot water held her captive, easing her strained muscles. But she finally dried off and slipped into clean clothes. Then she hurried downstairs.

Sally was already there, but she jumped to her feet to hug her cousin.

"I'm so glad you came. You've met Harriet?"

"Yes, I have. She convinced me to come to taste her apple pie."

"She had to convince you?" Penny demanded.

"No, not really. It was just a good excuse."

"Okay, I'll forgive you. Harriet, is there anything we need to do to help you?"

"No, just sit down. It's all ready," Harriet assured her, carrying dishes to the table. In no time, all three were enjoying Harriet's good cooking.

"So tell me, Penny, how's the new manager working out?"

"I don't know yet," Penny said, keeping her gaze on her plate.

"What do you mean?" Sally asked.

"Well, we've spent the last two days riding the perimeter of the property and he's been asking me lots of questions. The thing is I don't have too many answers."

"I thought he was supposed to be teaching you."

"I thought so, too, but I suppose he has to get to know the place first. I loaned him Dad's journals hoping that might help him, but I'm afraid he's going to get them destroyed."

"Why?" both Harriet and Sally demanded.

"Because when he told some of the men that he was reading Dad's journals, he said several of them looked alarmed, as if afraid they might have been mentioned in them. I'm just worried that the books won't be there when he returns."

"Didn't he hide them somewhere or do anything about safeguarding them?" Sally asked.

"He said he put the books somewhere safe, but who knows where that might be. I just wish I'd waited a while before handing them over." As if to underline her feelings, there was a knock on the back door. Penny got up to answer it.

"Penny," Jake said, "I'm sorry to interrupt your dinner, but I wanted to give these back to you before they are damaged. I think someone was in my room today while we were out. Luckily they didn't get to the books, but given time, they might."

Penny took the journals from him and

realized that she had been wrong about Jake. She suddenly felt rather guilty for her earlier outburst in front of Sally and Harriet. "But how are you going to read them to learn about the ranch?"

"I think they will be safer with you, but I thought maybe on Sunday, you'd let me come to the house and read them."

"Yes, of course."

There was a slight pause as Jake prepared to take his leave. But suddenly Penny wanted him to stay for just a little longer. "Did you get your dinner, Jake?"

"No, I slipped out while they were all getting in line. I'll get some food when I get back."

Harriet came to the door. "There's plenty of food here. Maybe you should ask Jake to join us."

Penny looked at Harriet. Then she turned back to Jake. "You can join us for dinner if you want. We have plenty."

"Are you sure you don't mind?"

"No, I don't mind. You must be hungry."

Once Jake stepped into the kitchen, he realized there was another guest. "I'm sorry. I didn't know you had company."

"Sally, this is Jake Larson, my manager. Jake, this is Sally Rogers, my cousin."

"It's nice to meet you, Sally. You run the general store, don't you?"

"Yes, I do."

Harriet put another place setting on the table. "Sit right here, Jake. Go ahead and serve yourself."

"This looks great, Harriet. I can see why Penny's pleased with your work."

"Why, thank you, Jake," Harriet said with a big smile.

Penny felt like everyone was smiling at Jake but her. "How could you tell someone had been in your room?"

Jake swallowed a mouthful of food before answering, "Well, a few things were moved around a little, not like I'd left them. I also found some scratch marks on the lock box that I'd stored the books in. There's no way that could've happened with it stored under my bed, so somebody has definitely been snooping around."

"When did they have time?"

"Cookie didn't say anything, but I believe some of them came in early. I intend to ask him about it when no one else is around."

"Have some rolls while they're hot," Harriet urged.

Jake took several rolls and began eating. Penny wanted to ask more questions, but she'd been raised by her mother's rules of etiquette. It was rude to interrupt a hungry man's meal.

When Harriet brought out her apple pie, Jake's eyes glowed. "Man, that looks good, Harriet."

"I hope it tastes good, Jake."

She had no doubt about its taste when Jake finished. He raved about her pie.

"I'll have to make some more for the bunkhouse, too. But I thought I'd make a cake next. I don't want you boys to get bored with the same dessert."

"We'll look forward to anything you send us, Harriet." Jake wiped his mouth with his napkin and put it beside his plate.

Again, Penny noted his good manners and felt a little pang for not trusting him more. But that didn't mean he hadn't risked her dad's journals by mentioning them to the cowboys.

He stood and thanked Harriet and Penny for inviting him to join them. Then he told Sally how pleased he was to meet her.

Penny wondered if there was any attraction there. She guessed she had no problem with that. But the sudden thought of Jake and Sally together made Penny feel decidedly uncomfortable. Penny didn't know why she was feeling this way, since she hardly knew Jake. She realized that she must be more tired than she thought. She said good-night, hoping her emotions didn't show. The look in Jake's eyes told her she wasn't as successful as she'd hoped. Blushing slightly, she turned to meet Jake's chocolate gaze, "Tomorrow at seven?" she asked.

"Right. Good night, everyone."

Once the door had closed behind him, Sally said, "Well, I think he's very nice, Penny. He's charming and polite and I'm sure he will make a wonderful manager."

Penny sat back down at the table. "I don't know what to think. But I'm grateful to have Dad's journals back." Penny gently ran her hand over the cover of the journals, her mind a riot of thoughts and feelings. It had been surprising how easy it had been to relax with Jake over dinner and she found herself looking forward to the day ahead.

She picked up the journals. "Harriet, if anyone asks you, you never saw these journals.

"Sure, Penny. What are you going to do with them?"

"Dad had a safe put in because a lot of cowboys liked to be paid in cash. He didn't want to keep a large amount of money here without a place to keep it secure. I'll put the journals in there where they'll be nice and safe." Penny stood up from the table.

"Sally, will you come on up with me?"

"Okay."

Upstairs, Penny went to her parents' room and opened the safe. Inside, she moved aside some papers and stored the two books there. "I think there's room for more of the books. Would you bring them here from Dad's bedside table?"

"I'll be glad to. I see you haven't changed anything in here. I'd wondered."

"Have you cleaned out your parents' bedroom?" Penny asked.

"No. It just seems…so final."

"I know. Harriet has volunteered to clean out the clothes that I don't want, to give to charity so someone will use them."

"I suppose that's a good idea. Maybe I can do it a little bit at a time."

"If you like you could ask Harriet to come help you on Saturday."

"You won't need her?"

"No. I'm not working on Saturdays and it will be nice to have a day all to myself."

Sally took a deep breath. "Yes, I'll ask her. It would be hard to do it alone."

"I know. Come on, we'll ask her." Penny led the way down the stairs to the kitchen.

Once there, they discussed the possibility of Harriet helping Sally clear out her parents' clothes like she was doing for Penny. Harriet agreed.

Sally hugged Penny again to say goodbye. Penny walked her out to her car, telling her to be careful.

She stood in the dark, watching Sally drive away, feeling lonelier than she had in several days.

Turning around, she walked back into the house. "Harriet, if any of the cowboys come to the house, don't let them in. Tell them they have to wait until I'm home, no matter what reason they give you."

"Got it. Do you really think they'll come after those books?"

"I can't be sure but I think it's possible, especially after what Jake said tonight. They believe Dad wrote something they could be prosecuted for; I'm sure they'd love to get their hands on them."

"Oh, my. Maybe I'll bring my gun in here tomorrow and keep it handy when I answer the door."

"You have a gun?" Penny asked in surprise.

"Yes. You have to have protection when you live out of town. Sheriff can't always get here in time to save you. You'd better be able to protect yourself."

"I never thought of that. Dad had guns, of course, but I never worried about my safety. My dad was always here to look out for me, I've never felt scared here in my life."

Harriet looked at the younger girl fondly. "Penny, your daddy isn't here anymore to look out for you. You need to make sure you can protect yourself."

Penny sighed, "You're right Harriet. There's just so much to think about since he's gone. I never had to worry about anything like that before. I'll have to ask Jake to show me how, maybe I will…soon. Oh, Harriet, before I forget, Jake would like a sandwich tomorrow, too, please."

"I'll be glad to feed that man. He's good-lookin', isn't he?"

Penny didn't bother to answer that question. Yes, Jake was very handsome, but Penny knew he was a ladies' man and she was definitely not looking for a romance! Besides, she needed to learn from Jake if she was ever going to make her dad proud. Thinking about Jake Larson's brown eyes and big hands would only complicate things!

As she went upstairs, she thought about what Harriet had said about protecting herself. Penny'd never fired a weapon, and the thought of actually killing someone made her sick to her stomach. But she supposed that now she was alone it was something she had to seriously think about. She just didn't know.

Could she ask Jake to show her how to shoot a gun? She didn't know if he was good with guns or not or what he might say about her learning. Come to think of it, Penny was discovering that there was more and more that she didn't know about the man.

Jake found himself looking forward to another day spent with Penny, which alarmed him. He knew better than to mix romance with business. He straightened his shoulders and strode to the corral to saddle up before Penny got there.

He was going to be all business-like today.

Penny got to the corral after he had saddled both horses. "You saddled Stormy for me? That wasn't necessary."

"I got here early today. It's no big deal." He kept his gaze on the pasture outside the corral.

"Okay. Thank you. Oh, and here's your lunch."

"Thanks." He looked around to be sure none of the cowboys were in earshot. He'd sent them all on their way a few minutes ago, but he had doubts about some of them doing their jobs properly.

"Where are we going today?"

"We're going to check on the cowboys to be sure they're doing their jobs."

"Isn't that going to require a lot of riding?"

"Yeah. Too much for you?"

Penny bridled slightly at his tone. Why did he always think that she wasn't up to this? "No. I just wondered if we might not cover more ground if we used the four-wheeler."

"I didn't know you had a four-wheeler."

"It's in the second barn and is all ready to go."

"Okay, we'll take the four-wheeler and give our mounts a rest."

"Good. Don't forget to bring along your lunch," she reminded him as she began unsaddling Stormy.

When they had both released their horses and provided them with a little hay, they walked over to the second barn and took the cover off the four-wheeler. "I'm glad you have one of these. They can come in handy."

"I agree. Shall I drive?"

He gave her a sharp look. "I think I should drive. I know where the cowboys are supposed to be."

"All right." She didn't argue, but she had a feeling Jake didn't think she was capable of driving. Well there would be time enough to show him. Putting her lunch behind the front seat, she settled in the passenger side.

He backed the four-wheeler out of the barn and headed out.

After riding for ten minutes, Penny turned to face him. Nervously she said, "Jake, may I ask you something?"

CHAPTER FOUR

JAKE turned to stare at her, letting up on the gas pedal slightly. "Yes?"

"Can you shoot?"

He continued to stare at her, surprise on his face. That was not the question he had been expecting, but then what had been? he asked himself. He thought back to his pledge earlier not to mix romance with business and cleared his throat before answering. "Yeah, Penny, I can shoot."

"Um, will you teach me how?"

"Teach you, why?"

"So I can protect myself."

"You're wanting to become the local Annie Oakley?"

"No. But it never occurred to me that I might need to protect myself. Harriet said I should learn because the sheriff might not be able to get to the ranch in time to save me if anything did happen." After a moment's silence, she added, "I think she's right."

"Why didn't your dad teach you?" Jake asked, but part of him already knew the answer.

Penny sighed as memories of her father came flooding back. "Dad never wanted me to learn anything about ranching. He always told me that I was not to worry about things like that and I guess he never saw the need because I was usually with either him or my mother. But now I need to look after myself."

Jake mulled over what Penny had said. Teaching her to shoot would involve a lot of personal time. Shooting wasn't simple. He'd have to commit to spending time with her— alone. The thought made Jake a little uneasy. But the thought of Penny unprotected did, too.

"I suppose I could show you, but you would have to do what I feel is necessary. You can't just pop off a couple of shots and think you're trained."

"I understand that. I know it's not a simple thing. I'm not even sure I'll shoot at someone. But I think I should have that option."

"Okay. We'll start tomorrow."

"Tomorrow? I hadn't planned—"

"When did you want to learn? Next year?" Okay, so he'd sounded really sarcastic, but he was agreeing to teach her. What more did she want?

Penny sat back in her seat, "No. Tomorrow is fine."

"I take it you don't have a gun?"

"I have all of Dad's guns. I don't know what I should learn with."

"I'll take a look in the morning. Does he—I mean, do you know where he kept his bullets?"

"I don't know anything about what he has, except I do remember him taking a rifle with him when he was riding over the country we rode over yesterday, the more mountainous areas."

"Yeah, the men mentioned seeing some bears and mountain lions in that area. They all take their rifles when they're working out there. In fact, I suggest they take their rifles out with them every day."

"You do? Why?"

"You never know how far down some of the animals will come. Rain has been scarce this year. With that spring-fed lake, you probably draw more wildlife than most ranches."

"I never thought of that."

"That's some of the stuff I'm supposed to teach you."

"Oh."

Jake suddenly pointed to two small figures in the distance. "There are the first cowboys."

"What were they assigned to do?"

"To ride the fence line. Make sure there aren't any breaks in the fence, and if there are, repair them."

"Are they about where you thought they would be?"

"Yeah."

They rode down the hill in silence. When they got close, Jake slowed down so as not to scare their horses. "Everything okay, guys?"

"Sure, boss. We haven't found any problems yet."

"Good deal."

He waved as he turned the vehicle in another direction.

"What purpose did that serve?"

"It's important for all the men to know that they'll be checked on. Otherwise, some of them won't do the work."

"Doesn't that make your job more difficult?"

"Did you think being a manager was easy?" Jake asked, raising one eyebrow.

Penny was again annoyed at his attitude that she wasn't cut out for the job. The man was so frustrating! "Did the manager at Dexter's ranch check on you?"

"Yeah, when I first started working there. After a while we became friends and he found out I always did my job."

"So, after a while, you might not have to check on everyone?"

"Maybe. There are some of them that I'm not sure I'll ever trust."

"The ones who were upset about Dad's journals?"

"Yeah. They've been acting funny since I got here and I think your dad maybe noticed something."

"Can't you just fire them?"

"No, that would send a bad message to the other men."

Penny crossed her arms over her chest in frustration. "I think you should just fire them."

They hit a bump that threw Penny into Jake's shoulder. She shrieked and he slowed down, reaching for her.

"Are you okay?"

Penny pulled back from the close contact, shocked at the hardness of his rugged frame and the attraction she felt flare. "Yes I'm fine! I just forgot to hold on."

"Okay." He pushed down on the gas pedal.

"So are you going to do what I said?"

Again he eased up on the gas. "You mean fire them?"

"Yes. I don't want them on the ranch."

"Not until they give me a reason."

"But I'm the owner!"

"Yes, you are, but you hired me, not only to manage the ranch, but to teach you how to do that job. I'm not teaching you to fire someone because you want to, without good reason."

She again folded her arms over her chest, forgetting that she needed to hold on. "What if I give you a direct order?"

"Then you'd have to find another manager," he said simply, still driving rapidly over the hills. "You'd better hold on."

Penny stewed, though she did hold on. But she didn't know what to do. She knew she was being unreasonable. Her father had said once that he didn't fire a man without good reason.

But she didn't want men who had stolen from her father remaining on the ranch. She knew Jake was right, but she was tired of him treating her like a little girl who didn't know what she was doing. Her father had done that her whole life.

She said nothing else. She was mad at Jake but she knew if she sent him away, she might not be able to find another manager for the very reason he gave for not firing the cowboys. Word would get out that she fired people on a whimsy.

They came over a hill to find four men driving a herd of cows into the next pasture, farther away from the mountains.

"How are things going?" he asked the men.

"Good, boss. We should be through earlier than we thought. These cows are trained. You want us to do something else?"

"Nah, you've done a good job. Have an early night."

The four men cheered and thanked Jake. Penny looked at him out of the corner of her eyes, wondering if he'd planned that situation to prove a point.

After they drove off, she asked, "I suppose

you did that so you could show me how to manage men?"

He frowned and stared at her. Her bright blue eyes were shining with anger; she looked so pretty when she was mad. Then he growled, "No, I didn't! You hired me to show you how to do things on a ranch and that's what I'm doing. I don't play games. If you think you can do things any better then go ahead, but while I'm here things get done my way."

Penny blushed and remained silent as Jake's words sank in.

"I'm sorry, I just wondered."

"Have you decided to let me go? I'd like to know now."

"No! But I have the right to ask questions, Jake!"

"Get your lunch out and start eating," he snapped, not looking at her.

She thought about not eating just to irritate him, but that seemed childish. Taking her sandwich out, she took a bite and chewed it. Jake did the same thing, driving with one hand. Neither of them spoke.

Finally he stopped the four-wheeler and turned to face her. "Yes, you have the right to ask questions. But questions that include my character aren't appropriate. If you doubt my character then you should fire me, period."

"I don't doubt your character. But I couldn't help wondering. You gave them time off work, for no good reason."

"You're only talking about a couple of hours. It would be hard to get to another area to work for very long. It seemed counterproductive to add to their day."

"Oh."

"The next time I need a little extra work from them, they'll remember that they got some time off earlier. It's part of managing men."

"Okay, I understand that now, but you didn't explain it like that before."

"No, I didn't know I had to!" he exclaimed. He really was going to have to teach Penny everything!

Jake reached behind him and brought out the apple that Harriet had included in his lunch and bit into it, as if he were gnawing on her neck.

She did the same, completely irritated with the man. She'd *told* him he'd have to explain ranch management to her, so why was he getting so angry about everything? What was wrong with him?

The last group they checked on, three men of whom Jake had been suspicious, were not where they were supposed to be. Jake drove along the route they should've taken to return to the bunkhouse, but they didn't overtake anyone.

When they got back to the ranch, Jake told her he intended to question Cookie if he could do so without anyone noticing. He would come to the house to tell her what he found out.

Penny went to the house, anxious to talk to Harriet. She found the woman in the kitchen, calmly preparing dinner.

"Harriet, did you have any visitors today?"

"I sure did. A couple of hours ago, three of the cowboys came to the door. They said they were here to pick up some books you wanted them to read. I told them you hadn't left anything with me for them. They asked to come in and look for them. I told them no."

"Did they leave?"

"Only after some creative arguing. But I told them I was new on the job and I didn't want to risk being fired."

"Good. Thank you, Harriet."

There was a knock on the door and both women froze. Then Penny opened the door. She breathed a sigh of relief when Jake greeted her.

"Come in."

"Evening, Harriet," Jake said as he entered the kitchen.

"Evening, Jake. Do you want some coffee?"

"That would be great. I haven't gotten thawed out yet."

Harriet brought coffee for both of them. Then she said, "I can go to my room, if you want to talk in private."

"No, Harriet. You need to tell Jake what you told me," Penny said.

Those words got Jake's attention. "Well, Harriet?"

She told him about the three cowboys who came to the house.

"Did they go away?"

"Only after an argument."

"That's interesting. So either Cookie lied to me, or they snuck past the bunkhouse, to come to the main house. But where are they now?"

Penny frowned. "They aren't in the bunkhouse now? But we saw their horses in the pasture."

"Yeah, we did. What time exactly did they come to the house, Harriet?"

"It was 1:25. There's this show on television that I watch most days when I eat my lunch. I missed the last five minutes of the show to talk to them."

"Do you know their vehicles?" Jake asked Penny.

"No, I don't. Do you think they've left?"

"It's possible. And if they haven't left, then I have some questions to ask them." He took another drink of coffee.

"Why don't you stay for dinner, Jake? I have it ready and there's plenty," Harriet suggested.

"I ate your good cooking last night, Harriet. I don't want to impose on you or Penny."

Penny knew Harriet was looking at her, waiting for her to speak. She finally said, "You might as well stay. Then it won't look like you were checking on anyone. When you get back, maybe they'll be there, or their bunks may be cleared off."

"You're sure?" Jake asked, staring at Penny, his dark gaze locking with hers.

She shrugged her shoulders, blushing slightly. "Of course I'm sure. It'll be nice to have some company."

Harriet set another place and began putting dishes on the table.

Jake drew a deep breath, taking in the aroma of the meal. "I think this smells better than what Cookie is dishing up."

"I baked a cake for the bunkhouse to help out. And, of course, I baked a cake for here."

"That's really nice of you, Harriet. The comments I heard about your apple pies were rave reviews."

Harriet beamed. "I pride myself on my baking."

"Jake, if the men have left, will we be able to find replacements?" Penny asked, bringing the subject back to their situation.

"It won't be easy. Good cowboys are hard to find."

"What do we do? Put a sign on our gate that we need riders?"

"No. You put notices in the paper and on the bulletin board in the General Store. Your cousin's store."

"Sally's store, of course, I'd forgotten about that."

"It's a tough time to find riders. Most of them are hunkered down for the winter. There's not a lot of moving around at Christmas time."

"No, of course—oh, no! It's December. We have to find a Christmas tree for the town party. We supply one every year. How could I have forgotten that?"

"I didn't know the tree came from your place. I've seen it for several years. Pretty impressive." Jake smiled at her.

"We have to find a good tree and cut it down. They have to have the tree in time to decorate it for the party. We only have a week to find the perfect tree."

"Which cowboys usually take care of that job?"

Penny blinked quickly to dissipate the tears in her eyes. "Not the cowboys. Dad and I used to pick out the tree together. Then he would take several cowboys with him to cut it down and take it to town."

Jake could sense that this was a difficult subject for Penny. "How do you know he got the right tree?" he asked softly.

"I'd tie a red scarf on the tree we had chosen so that they could find it easily. We need to go look for it tomorrow."

Harriet sat down at the table, ready for them to eat. "I don't think you can go tomorrow."

"Why not?" Penny demanded.

"We're supposed to have a snowstorm tomorrow. Maybe a foot of snow. Let's say the prayer so we can eat. The food will get cold."

Penny quickly said the prayer her parents had always said before each meal. Then Harriet started passing the dishes first to Jake and then to Penny.

"Good thing we moved that herd today. They'll be easier to feed. I don't think the storm is supposed to last too long, is it, Harriet?" Jake asked.

"The weatherman said it would blow through by early afternoon."

"Will the cowboys work on Saturday to feed the herds?" Penny asked.

"Of course they will. Saturday is a workday." Jake took a bite of food.

Penny did the same as she thought about Jake's response. She didn't consider Saturday a workday. Clearly she still had a lot to learn.

"Your dad had it set up that half the cowboys worked on Saturday and half on Sunday. But they all know that they may be called upon to work extra hours if the weather is bad. The storm is supposed to start before sunrise."

Harriet nodded. "I think they said it would start about 4:00 a.m."

"Good. The cowboys will hunker down until the storm stops. I'll get them to feed the herds before they leave the ranch."

"What else do they have to do?"

"Break the ice in the water tanks. We shouldn't have any mamas due this early, but they'll check the herds for any cows in distress."

"Okay, what time will we start?"

"The cowboys and I will go out as soon as the storm stops. I don't think you should ride out tomorrow."

Penny straightened her shoulders and stared at Jake. "Dad always rode with the staff. He never stayed inside just because of a storm. Besides, if those three men are missing, you'll be short-handed."

Jake kept his gaze on his food. "We'll manage."

"Not without me. I'll be ready when the storm stops."

"Have you ever been outside for a long ride in weather that is that cold?"

"Not for a long time, but I can bundle up as much as anyone can."

"I think women require more heat! You'll freeze to death and you'll complain constantly."

Penny glared at her manager. "You're being ridiculous! And have you heard me complain once?"

"No, but that doesn't mean you might not complain tomorrow. It's going to be bitterly cold."

"You both better eat your dinner before *it's* bitterly cold," Harriet reminded them.

"Right, Harriet," Jake said with a grateful smile.

Penny did as Harriet suggested, too, but she wasn't particularly grateful for the reminder. She didn't intend to let Jake have his way. She intended to do her job as owner of her ranch and he was meant to be teaching her how to manage it. Besides, he had no right to treat her like a three-year-old. She was an adult! Once again she felt as though she was being wrapped in cotton wool and it annoyed her. She needed to prove to Jake that she was up to the job at hand.

When the meal was over, Harriet brought out her cake. It was beautiful and tasted even better. Penny watched Jake eat his cake. It was a true lesson on how to enjoy a dessert. She felt an unexpected heat rising in her body and quickly looked away.

When Jake finished his dessert, he thanked Harriet and then got up and carried his plate and glass to the sink.

"Here now, you don't have to do that!" Harriet protested as she jumped up to follow him.

"My mama insisted everyone carried their dishes to the sink."

"Well, she raised you right," Harriet said with a smile.

Penny brought her dishes to the sink, too. Then she went back to bring the serving plates. Jake immediately joined her.

"I can do this, Jake."

"I'll help," he said and ignored her irritated look.

"I'll accept your help, as long as you accept my help tomorrow."

"Penny, tomorrow is different. It will be very cold and there's no need."

"Jake I'm owner of this ranch now and my dad always went," she insisted, raising her chin as she stared at him.

Jake took a deep breath and slowly released it as he looked Penny straight in the eyes. "Being stubborn isn't always the best thing. Maybe that's the first thing you need to learn." Then he said good-night and went out the back door.

"Ooh! He makes me so mad!" Penny exclaimed, staring after him.

"I think he's right. You should stay home tomorrow and stay warm. Just because your dad did things doesn't mean you have to do them, too. You have to find your own way, Penny. Besides, you'll get cold enough when you go out to find the perfect tree tomorrow."

Penny sat down at the table and rested her head in her hands. "Oh, I suppose you're right. I can't learn everything all at once and I am so tired. Maybe Jake's right. He'd planned to start my shooting lessons in the morning. I guess that will have to be postponed, too."

"I'm glad you're going to learn to protect yourself."

"Me, too. I should've showed Jake Dad's guns while he was here."

Harriet smiled to herself as she glanced across at Penny seated at the table. "Oh, I'm sure he'll be back. He's a man who clearly enjoys his meals."

"Yes, he does," Penny agreed, remembering watching him eat his piece of cake.

For once, the weatherman was accurate.

Jake had noted the absence of the three cowboys. Their personal areas had been cleaned out. Cookie admitted that they had come back to the bunkhouse and packed up in the afternoon, but they'd sworn to hurt him if he let Jake know before dark.

"It's okay, Cookie. I was pretty sure they had gone."

This morning, he'd organized his remaining staff. They had to feed three different herds, break the ice on the water supply and check for any cows in distress. He had eight men, including himself. Jake divided the men into two groups of three and he took Dusty, the best cowboy, to be with him.

After lunch, he warned all of them to wrap

up as much as possible. "It's going to be cold out there. Once you've finished your assigned tasks, get back here as soon as possible. Cookie will have a pot of coffee on the stove. First ones back can build a fire in the fireplace, too."

They were all bundling up when a knock on the door brought them all to a halt.

Jake knew who it was. He didn't want to answer the knock, but he couldn't leave her out there in the cold. He swung open the door. "Get in here!" he ordered stiffly.

Penny stepped into the bunkhouse.

CHAPTER FIVE

ALL the cowboys greeted Penny and she smiled at them. But her smile faded when it reached Jake. He was glaring at her. "What are you doing here?" he demanded.

"I told you I'd come help. You don't have enough men to handle three herds. I'll even out the numbers."

"No. I want you to go back to the house and stay warm."

"No, I won't. I'm dressed warm enough."

"No!"

"Yes!"

"Uh, boss, I think we'll be able to do the job faster with three of us. We can take a truck and she can do the driving while we feed the herd and make sure they've got water," Dusty suggested.

Everyone waited for Jake's reply. Finally he turned toward Penny and said, "Can you drive a truck?"

"Of course I can." Penny smiled and sent a grateful look at Dusty.

Jake glared even harder at Penny. He didn't want her flirting with any of his men! "All right. Let's go." He zipped up his jacket and grabbed his gloves. "We'll take my truck."

He handed the keys to Penny. "It's the blue one parked outside."

"You want me to drive now?" Penny asked in surprise.

"Yeah." He held open the door.

Penny moved out into the frigid air, clutching the key in her gloved hands.

"Drive the truck over to the hay barn. We'll load in some bales of hay."

Jake jumped in the back of his truck, along with Dusty, and sat on the edge of the truck bed while Penny drove to the hay barn. When they got there, he and Dusty loaded the bales of hay they would need for the day ahead. When they were through, both men got in the cab of the truck with Penny. Jake sat in the middle.

"Okay, let's go."

They drove over some rough land that threw the three of them together. Jake tried to brace himself so he wouldn't land against Penny's soft body. She had the heater turned on full force and he reached over to turn it down.

"You're not cold?" Penny asked in amazement.

"Yeah, we're cold," he responded, "but we're going to have to go out into even colder temperatures in a few minutes. It's easier to adjust if we don't sweat in all we've got on."

"Oh, I'm sorry. I didn't think of that."

"Don't worry about it."

They remained silent the rest of the way. When they reached the pasture, they found the herd huddled in the southeast corner, their backs to the snowstorm. Penny came to a halt near the herd and beat on the horn. At the same time, both men got out of the truck and jumped into the back. They began clipping the wires on the bales and breaking them into smaller pieces as they threw the hay out to the cows.

Penny began to drive slowly so the hay would be spread out and more cows could reach the feed. When there was just a couple of bales left, Dusty jumped off the truck and ran to the tank that provided water for the herd.

With an ax he worked on cutting the ice so the cows could have water.

While feeding the herd, Jake had been looking for any cows that might be down, but they all seemed to be in good shape. When Jake finished the last of the hay, he jumped off the back of the truck and opened the passenger door, getting in.

"Okay, let's go pick up Dusty."

Penny pressed on the gas, moving the truck over the rough ground, bouncing more since the weight of the hay had been removed. In a couple of minutes, they reached the tank and Jake jumped out.

"I got it," Dusty called, moving to the truck. "Are we all done?"

"Yeah, come on. The heater is going good."

Penny looked at Jake in surprise. He'd turned the heater down when they started out. Did that mean he wanted it on high for the trip back?

"Yeah, I want you to crank it up now."

She did so, but she wondered if he'd read her mind. That made her feel very nervous.

When Penny parked Jake's truck, she removed the key and handed it to him. She had been unsure as to whether to come and help the men today, but now felt proud of her involvement in the day's work. It sure was a nice feeling.

Jake slid out of the truck, telling Penny to wait a minute. She came around the truck to see what he wanted. He was talking to Dusty, so she waited patiently.

When he finished his conversation with Dusty, he came to Penny's side and took her arm, pulling her toward the house.

"What are you doing, Jake? I can manage to get to the house by myself."

"No, I'm escorting you, and when we get inside, we're having a little talk."

Both anger and fear rose in Penny. What was wrong with the man? She'd helped him out this morning. Didn't he appreciate it?

Once they reached the house, the warm air surrounding them, Jake removed his hold from her arm. They were barely inside the kitchen when he started laying down the law.

"Penny, you hired me to be the boss here! I expect you to mind me and not argue in front of the men! They'll never respect me when you get the better of me in an argument!"

He paused to draw breath, she supposed, but she took the opportunity to have her say. "What century do you think you're living in? I'm the boss here, and I always will be! I argued with you today because you were wrong!"

"Then I'm sorry, Penny, but I can't be your manager!" Jake exclaimed and turned to leave.

Before he could disappear, Harriet appeared from further in the kitchen and stuck a mug of hot coffee in his hands. "Jake, now don't go out in the cold without something hot inside you," she said calmly.

"Harriet, I can't—"

"Yes, you can. Penny, here's your coffee. Now, it seems to me that the two of you need to have a rational discussion before Jake loses a job he really likes, and you, Penny, lose a good, honest manager."

Both Penny and Jake opened their mouths to protest, but then they did as Harriet said and sat down at the table. Harriet went to the oven and pulled out a pan of biscuits and sausage.

"This will give you something to chew on," the housekeeper said, putting saucers in front of each of them.

"Man, Harriet, you really know how to make us feel good," Jake said, taking a bite of the warm food.

"Thank you, Harriet," Penny added. She knew Harriet was right. Losing a good manager just because they had a difference of opinion was crazy.

After eating in silence for a few minutes, Penny said, "I'm sorry I argued with you in front of the men. But you shouldn't have shut me out! It is my ranch, Jake, and I need to learn about what must be done."

"You shouldn't have argued in front of the men, but we'll let that slide. As for coming out with us today I was just trying to protect you, Penny. I think that's what your dad would've wanted!"

"Jake, my dad spent his whole life protecting me, but he isn't here any longer. I have to learn how to survive on my own now."

Silence fell and Penny had tears in her eyes. Jake bowed his head, wanting to take her into his arms, but knowing he couldn't.

Finally he looked at Penny. "You're right, Penny. I was wrong in trying to keep you inside. You did do a great job in helping us. I'll do a better job of teaching you about ranching." Jake reached over the table and took Penny's small hand in his own, stroking her delicate skin with his thumb. He stared into her eyes and realized that seeing her cry was the last thing he wanted. He brushed away a tear from her face with his other hand. "I'm sorry, Penny," he said softly.

"Thank you, Jake," Penny whispered. She felt a tingling deep in her stomach and when she looked up and met Jake's hard glaze, she felt desire flare. Penny quickly pulled her hand away, jumped up and ran out of the kitchen.

Jake stared at the door through which she'd disappeared.

Harriet appeared and touched Jake gently on the shoulder. "She's all right, but she's remembering her parents right now. It's hard on her."

"Yeah. She seems so young, it's hard to remember that she's all grown up, ready to take over the job of owning a ranch."

"I know. But she's stronger than you realize. It will just take a while to learn to deal with everything."

"Yeah. Thanks for calming us down."

"I'm glad I could help."

"These biscuits and sausage helped, too," Jake added with a smile.

Harriet urged him to take another one. He did

so and then excused himself. When he got back to the bunkhouse, all the men were there having cups of coffee, sitting around the fire.

Jake paused, but then he said what needed to be said. "I was wrong today, trying to force Penny to stay inside. I forgot that she's trying to learn to manage the ranch, like her dad did. I've got to teach her about ranching, and that includes cold days like today."

His men all consoled him, offering comments on the difficulty of managing a ranch and a woman. Jake was glad Penny wasn't there to hear their comments. "We have to remember that she's the owner of the ranch," he added.

"Hell, boss, we know that, but it seems wrong for a pretty little girl like Penny to be out in the cold," one cowboy said.

"Wrong or not, Penny is the boss, and we all need to remember that, me especially," Jake said, remembering just how pretty Penny had looked as he'd sat and held her hand.

Sunday morning, Penny dressed to go to church with Harriet. She didn't think to volunteer for work. It was only when they were leaving for the small church in Bailey that it occurred to her that the men would be doing the same job as yesterday.

"Don't even think about it," Harriet said. "Let them handle things today."

"But Harriet, Dad would've—"

"I know, Penny, but you need to go to church this morning."

"Yes, I do. I think it will help me. And Sally is expecting to see me there."

"Maybe she'd like to come home with us for Sunday dinner," Harriet suggested.

"That's a lovely idea. I'll ask her."

But Sally couldn't come, telling Penny how much work she had to do that afternoon to be ready for Christmas in Bailey. "You haven't forgotten about the tree, have you, Penny?"

"Of course not. Dad and I—yes, Jake will help me." She hugged her cousin and hurried back to Harriet's side ready to return to the ranch.

When they got there, they had only stepped inside when a knock sounded on the back door. Penny opened it to find Jake bundled up, standing there. He looked tall and rugged in the open doorway and Penny again felt that unfamiliar tingling sensation run down her spine.

"Hi, Jake. Come in."

"I thought we'd better locate the tree you're wanting to cut down for Christmas."

"Yes, I do, but I haven't eaten lunch yet. Do you think it could wait for, say, half an hour?"

"Yeah, I guess. I'll come back then."

Harriet, behind Penny, said, "Why don't you join us for lunch?"

"No, I couldn't—"

Suddenly desperate for Jake to stay a little longer, Penny echoed Harriet. "Please, Jake? There's plenty to spare."

Jake hesitated, still trying to figure out what had happened between him and Penny last night, if anything. But the smell of Harriet's cooking was too good to refuse and he nodded his head and stepped into the warmth of the kitchen.

"You'd better take your coat off so you don't get overheated," Harriet said as she hurriedly set another plate.

"Harriet, I don't need to eat. Cookie served lunch a little while ago," Jake explained.

"You can just nibble a little then while Penny eats."

But soon Jake was eating just as much as Penny.

"Will we use the four-wheeler for our search?"

"I think that will work best. Is it okay with you?"

"Yes, that's—that's the way we always do it." Penny ducked her head but she remained in her seat. In a minute, she'd conquered the tears.

Harriet smiled at her encouragingly and said softly, "Good girl."

Penny smiled at her. Her housekeeper was filling the roles of both her father and her mother. She was lucky to have Harriet in her life. And Jake.

Jake noticed how difficult it was for Penny to talk about the tree expedition and he was impressed with how strong she was being. "What area did you find the tree in last year?" he asked.

Penny turned to face Jake. "We always go to the same area, in the north pasture. Toward the western edge, there's a forest that has some beautiful trees."

"Okay, sounds good to me." Jake wiped his mouth with his napkin. "You about ready?"

"Yes, I just need to put on some heavier clothes—we could be gone for some time."

* * *

"This one looks pretty good," Jake said hopefully. They'd been looking at trees for at least half an hour after a bone-chilling ride in the four-wheeler. He was just about ready to head for home.

"No, its trunk is too crooked." Penny continued to look at the trees around them.

"Come on, Penny, we've been looking for a while now and my feet are pretty much frozen."

"Jake, the tree has to be—there! There it is."

Jake stared at the trees, not seeing what Penny was seeing. "Where?"

"There, the tallest one." She reached in her pocket for a red scarf she'd brought with her. "Come on. Let's go tie the red scarf on it." She jumped in the four-wheeler, waiting for Jake to join her.

"Where are we going?" Jake asked, still confused.

"Maybe I should drive," she said, moving over to the driver's side. She started the engine and Jake joined her hurriedly before he got left behind.

When they reached the tree she'd selected, Jake held his breath that she didn't change her mind. They'd chosen some other trees that had failed her test when they got close.

"Oh, yes," she said, after she'd walked all the way around the tree. "This is the perfect tree!"

Jake felt a sudden burst of pleasure that they had found the one Penny wanted, but not just because his feet were quickly turning into blocks of ice. The look on Penny's face spoke volumes and Jake suddenly understood how important this had been for her. He also realized that in asking him to come along he had replaced the role of her dad and he felt an odd sensation in his chest. He quickly brushed his feelings aside not wanting to think about exactly what that meant.

"Where shall I tie the scarf, Jake?" Penny asked, her blue eyes bright.

Jake brought himself back to the job at hand and cleared his throat. "Well, the higher the better. Do you want me to tie it?"

"No, Dad always—no, that's my job." She stretched up as high as she could and tied the red scarf on the end of a branch that would be highly visible.

"There. Will you be able to see it when you come back to cut it down?" Penny asked.

"Why? Aren't you coming with us?"

"No, I—yes, I am. You're right. I should come with you." She nodded her head.

"Then I reckon you'll be able to find that red scarf."

They both stood for a moment looking at the magnificent tree in front of them. Neither of them spoke and the silence stretched. Finally Penny let out a deep breath and smiled up at Jake.

"You're right, Jake, I'll be able to find this tree again with my eyes closed."

Monday morning, the frigid temperatures had turned to a balmy thirty-eight degrees and the snow was melting in the sunny spots. When Penny appeared at the barn, Jake was already there, but he hadn't saddled the horses.

"We're going to start your shooting lessons today."

"We are?"

"Yeah, your first lesson is today. We need to go look at your dad's guns."

Penny sighed. "I'm not sure my shooting lessons should come before ranching duties."

"The men are all doing the ranching jobs,

and I trust them to do their jobs since the other three have taken off. So now is the time to start your shooting lessons. Okay?"

"Okay." Penny had to admit that she wasn't as enthusiastic about it as she had been. She didn't feel threatened in her own home, especially after those cowboys had left, so maybe she didn't need to learn anymore. But she couldn't tell Jake she changed her mind, he would be angry with her for wasting his time and she'd vowed to be more agreeable with him.

She led the way back to the house, telling Harriet what they were doing. Her father's guns were locked in a case in the den. Penny found the key and unlocked the wall case.

Jake selected a rifle.

"We want to start with a rifle? Wouldn't a pistol be easier?" Penny asked.

"No. This is the best weapon for us to start with. Come on."

A few minutes later, they were standing in a low-lying pasture facing a hill just behind the house. Penny was holding the rifle Jake had chosen. He'd just shown her how to load it and now he was directing her on the proper way to shoot.

Penny swung around to face him, holding the rifle as he had shown her, which meant the barrel was pointed directly at him.

He grabbed the barrel of the rifle and pointed the gun straight in the air. "Damn it, woman, are you trying to kill me?"

Penny stared at him, her mouth open. His glare woke her from her trance. "Of course not! Why would you think such a thing?"

"You just pointed the rifle straight at me!"

"But I just wanted to ask you—"

"Rule number one: You never point the barrel at a person unless you intend to harm him!"

"Fine!" Penny shouted, sure he was making a big deal about nothing. She turned and started marching toward the house, refusing to listen to his tirade.

"Penny, are you going to quit on this already or are you going to get back here and finish the job!"

That stopped her. She turned to stare at him. "Why should I, Jake? I didn't intend to hurt you and you know it."

Jake took a step toward her. "I'm sorry I yelled at you. But shooting isn't a game and that's a rule you can't break. You don't ever point a rifle at anyone unless you intend to shoot him."

Penny sighed. "Okay, but I guess I'm not as interested in shooting as I once was."

"You need to learn, Penny."

She knew he was right and started back toward him.

When she reached him, he held out the rifle. Reluctantly she took it.

"Now, bring the gun up and line it up with the target. Put your finger on the trigger. When you fire there will be a little kick, so hold the gun tightly. Now, squeeze the trigger."

She pulled the trigger, but she didn't hit the target.

She lowered the rifle and looked at Jake.

"You missed."

"I know that! Why did I miss it? I did what you said."

"You didn't hold the gun tight enough."

"Yes, I did!"

"No, you didn't. Look," he said, putting his hands on hers, which meant she was practically standing in his embrace. His arms were big and strong around Penny's shoulders and his mouth was right by her ear. As he spoke she felt his warm breath featherlight against her cheek and a shiver ran along her spine. "Try it again," he said quietly.

This time she hit the target.

"You see?" he said, stepping back from her, suddenly breathing deeply. "You hit it."

Penny couldn't quite manage to respond. She was too struck by the coldness that surrounded her once Jake had removed his arms from around her. Penny straightened herself and tried not to look at Jake, instead she fiddled with the rifle.

"Do you need to walk over and look at the mark?" Jake asked.

"No. I—I think we should try it again."

"*You* should try it again—without me." When Penny didn't move, he gestured with his hand. "Go ahead. Try it again."

Penny slowly raised the rifle. She tried to replicate the steadiness Jake had demonstrated, but it was difficult. She took aim and squeezed the trigger.

"You did it!" Jake shouted proudly. "You hit the target."

"Are you sure?" Penny asked in amazement.

"Yes, I'm sure. Good job, Penny."

"Th-thank you, I guess."

"Try another shot. This time aim for the top of the target, where it's thinner." He'd set up a piece of cardboard against a tree that narrowed at the top.

Penny frowned, but she brought the rifle up to her cheek and clutched it tightly. Then she squeezed the trigger.

"Try again, Penny. You weren't far off."

Again she squeezed the trigger.

"Great! You hit it. You're a natural." Jake came over to Penny and instinctively put his arm around her shoulder to congratulate her. Again Penny found herself enfolded in Jake's strong embrace and wanted nothing more than to hold on tight. As an uncomfortable silence fell between them, Jake suddenly released his hold and began to busy himself setting up another target.

"Okay, good job! Now we'll try—"

"Jake, I'm tired of shooting. Can't this be enough for today?"

"But, Penny, you have so much more to learn," Jake said, staring at her.

"It's easier when you help me," she pointed out, waiting for his reaction.

Jake was silent for a moment and looked at his boots intently. "I—I could probably help you again, if that's what you want."

"Yes, I think I'll learn better that way." She held her breath, hoping he'd touch her again. When he moved in close and put his arms around her, she let out that breath. His warmth surrounded her and she leaned back just a little, where she felt his chest against her back.

"You are paying attention, aren't you?" Jake asked, his voice above her. He sounded suspicious, as if he'd figured out what she wanted.

"Yes, I'm paying attention."

"Okay, line up your sight. Aim for the lower right side of the target."

Penny did so and even she was pleased when she realized she'd hit the target where she'd aimed. "I hit it!"

"Yes, you did," Jake said, smiling at her. "But I think you need to do it on your own now."

The enthusiasm she'd felt momentarily disappeared. "But—"

"But you need to do it on your own."

Penny's cheeks heated up. She didn't want to admit that his touch was becoming important to her. That wasn't part of the deal. She'd asked him to teach her, as she believed her father would've done. But Jake didn't feel like her father; he felt hard and strong and he made her feel safe and protected in a way even she had never felt before.

CHAPTER SIX

HARRIET looked up as Penny walked into the
kitchen.

"Is something wrong?"

"No. I just got cold during shooting practice.
I'm going to stay in for the rest of the day."

Harriet walked over and felt of Penny's face.
"Are you sure you're feeling okay?"

"Yes, I'm fine, but there is so much to do
around here. I need to get out the ornaments for
our—oh, no! We haven't gotten a tree for the
house yet."

"I thought maybe you didn't want to do a tree
this year, so I hadn't said anything."

"We have to have a tree. We always have
one." Penny sat down at the table.

"There's still time. Maybe you and Jake can go
on another tree search," Harriet said with a smile.

"No! No, I'll—I'll call the bunkhouse. Maybe Cookie hasn't left yet."

She ignored Harriet's strange look and reached for the phone. "Cookie? It's Penny. Would you please tell Jake that I need a Christmas tree for the house? As soon as possible. Thank you."

After she hung up the phone, she sat there staring into the distance.

"Penny, are you sure you're feeling all right?"

"Yes, but—but it will seem so strange, just you and me decorating the tree. We always used to make a big occasion out of doing it— a real family tradition you know?" Penny's eyes filled with tears as she thought back to the happy times spent with her family.

Harriet gently took Penny's hand and stroked it. "Well, it seems to me that you have a new family now and you need to start making some new traditions. Why don't you invite the men in to help you decorate the tree and I'll cook for all of them."

"That would be a lot of work, Harriet."

"Nonsense. It would just be a small party. I'll be delighted to cook for them, we could do it tomorrow night."

"Thank you. It's a wonderful idea and I would never have thought of it. Oh, I know! I'll get them each a present and we can play that gift exchange game."

"Oh, I played that one year. It's a lot of fun."

"I'll call Sally and get her to pick out eight gifts. Then I can go in and pick them up. That way I can help you get ready."

"Won't Jake need you to—"

"No! He won't want me to do anything," Penny answered, a little too quickly.

"Did you two have another argument?"

"Not exactly. Now, I'd better go find those ornaments."

Penny hurried from the room before Harriet asked her any more questions about her afternoon with Jake. Penny still hadn't thought about exactly what had happened between them during the shooting practice, but she decided she had far too many other things to do before that. In the back of the storage closet at the top of the stairs she found the huge box of Christmas ornaments she was looking for.

Next to the decorations, Penny found some boxes already wrapped in Christmas paper and labeled for her father. Slowly Penny opened the gifts that would have been handed over by her dear mother on Christmas Day and couldn't help feeling an immense sadness wash over her. In the boxes she discovered a new pair of dress boots and a cashmere neck scarf and matching gloves.

Penny had no idea what to do with the gifts, neither would be appropriate for the cowboys. The boots would have cost far more than she'd intended to spend, and the scarf and gloves were not something any of the cowboys would normally wear.

She also found a number of gifts to her. Penny was tempted to open them, but she decided to wait until Christmas morning. She took those boxes to her bedroom. Then she carried the ornaments into the den, to await the Christmas tree.

"Did you find everything?" Harriet asked as Penny returned to the kitchen.

"Yes, I did," Penny said.

"Have you been crying?"

Penny laughed a little. "Yes, I thought I'd wiped my tears away. I found some Christmas presents my mom had already bought and wrapped up."

"That must've been difficult."

"Yes, it was. I opened what she'd bought my dad, but I saved my presents for Christmas morning."

"That'll be nice. What are you going to do with your dad's presents?"

"I don't know, they won't work for the cowboys, but that reminds me, I'm going to call Sally now. I think she can find gifts for them."

She made the call and Sally assured her she could find presents in the price range Penny suggested.

After she hung up the phone, Penny said, "She sounded awfully busy. I hope I'm not making too much work for her."

"I'm sure she'll manage. Who are you going to get to pick up the gifts? And will they be already wrapped?"

"I'll pick them up when I go into town for the groceries we'll need for tomorrow night. I need to start making a list. Have you thought about what you want to serve?"

They were soon engrossed in making a menu and a grocery list that took almost until lunchtime.

* * *

That night after dinner, there was a knock on the bunkhouse door. Jake moved to open it, hoping it might be Penny.

It was Penny at the door, but she explained that she'd come to talk to everyone, not just Jake. He stood back and let her enter.

She moved next to the fire, in front of everyone. With a smile, she said, "As you all know, my parents were—were killed in a car crash and this will be my first Christmas without them. We always had a Christmas tree when they were alive and I want to continue that tradition, but—but it seems rather lonely with just Harriet and me decorating it. So I wondered if you'd all like to help me. We could have a tree decorating party tomorrow night, since Jake delivered a beautiful tree to the house today. Would that be all right with everyone?"

The men exchanged glances with each other, all a little uncomfortable with Penny's request, but slowly, one by one, they all agreed to help. Jake breathed a sigh of relief knowing that the speech Penny had just made had been difficult for her.

"Harriet promises to make you a great

dinner, which means Cookie gets a night off, and I'll provide the decorations. Any special requests?"

They assured her Harriet's cooking would be great, especially Cookie.

"Then we'll expect you tomorrow evening around six?" She looked at Jake for confirmation and he nodded his head. "Oh, and the dress is casual. No tuxes required and finally, thanks everyone, this really means a lot to me."

With a small smile she excused herself, after again thanking them for being so agreeable, and left, without a single word to Jake.

There was a moment of silence before Dusty said, "Hell, I'd have posed for the tree itself if she asked me to, poor girl. This must be really hard on her."

There was agreement from all the cowboys. Jake knew exactly how they felt. He guessed maybe he'd been too hard on Penny that morning, though he didn't know exactly why. He couldn't think of anything he'd done. *He'd* been a little upset about putting his arms around her. Knowing he'd done it to steady the rifle, he'd told himself he was being ridiculous. But he'd moved away as quickly as possible, before she'd noticed.

But tomorrow night they'd help her through the tree decorating, and get a good meal from Harriet. It would be a nice thing. It would remind him of being at home for Christmas. It had been a while since he'd done that.

"Okay, tomorrow everyone come in by five. Penny said dress casual, but we all want to be sure to clean up. And use your best manners."

"Aw, boss, we know that," Cookie assured him. "Just don't forget what napkins are for," he added, looking sternly at his friends.

They laughed and assured him they wouldn't.

All the next day Penny worked in the kitchen with Harriet.

"We work well together. I didn't realize you were such a good cook, Penny," Harriet said.

"Yes, I enjoy cooking, but I figured I wouldn't have the time or energy if I spent all day outside."

"I wouldn't think so. Ranching's hard work, especially when you're not used to it. Not that cooking isn't, but it takes more mental stress, I always say."

"Maybe so, but I enjoy it."

"I like those pinwheel ham and cheese things you made. I bet they just fly off the plate."

"I'm sure they will since we're putting them out first, along with the nachos. I'm glad you thought of those. That beef sure does smell good."

"Thank you. I thought about supplying ham and cheese sandwiches, too, but these are cowboys. They like beef."

"I think you're right. And then they can stuff themselves on dessert. With cake, pie and iced brownies, they'll have plenty to choose from."

"Well, we want them to enjoy themselves."

"Yes, we do. Did I tell you I bought candy canes for the tree? I love those."

"Me, too. And Jake picked out a beautiful tree. Did you thank him?"

Penny considered her words from the night before. "Yes, I did." Not exactly but close enough.

"What are you going to wear tonight?"

Penny looked at Harriet in surprise. "Wear? My regular clothes, I guess."

"I think you should put on nice pants and a sweater. After all, you're the hostess. I'm going to put on a dress, but I'm wearing one of the prettiest aprons."

"You're right, Harriet. After all, I would at least wear that if I invited anyone else to the house."

"Well, you'd better go dress soon. It's almost five o'clock."

"Oh, my! I had no idea it was so late. It won't take me more than half an hour, but I have to have a shower before I get dressed."

"All right. I'll turn the oven down low and go get dressed myself." They both rushed from the kitchen.

When the knock came on the back door, everything was ready. Penny had built a fire in the fireplace and the pinwheels she'd made were on the coffee table, a plate at each end.

Harriet put the first trays of nachos in the oven. They'd be ready by the time all the men found a place to sit. Penny had pushed several chairs alongside the couch and two matching chairs.

Swinging wide the door, she greeted them with a smile, welcoming them to her home. They followed her to the den, but they gazed longingly at the kitchen, looking for something to eat. She invited them to sample the hors d'oeuvres.

One of the cowboys whispered something,

but before she could ask what he wanted, the man next to him whispered something that put him at ease.

Harriet's entry with the nachos cheered everyone up. Then one of them tasted the pinwheels and assured everyone they were great. Penny took the empty nacho trays back to the kitchen. Harriet had the other two trays just about ready to be served. Penny waited and carried them in.

"Don't eat too many of the nachos and pinwheels, because Harriet has a great dinner planned. Oh, and you should see the desserts," she added with a big smile.

The men all cheered at the thought of more good food, but getting out the ornaments quietened them all down. Penny didn't know if they were remembering past Christmases or if they were worried about breaking the ornaments. She smiled at them, hoping to put them at ease.

"I've already put the lights on the tree. The first decoration that has to go on is the Christmas star. It goes on top. Who is the tallest?"

All the men looked at Jake. Penny had guessed he'd be the one. He was tall, like her dad. He stood and took the star she was holding from her. Without a word, he put the star in place. Afterward he looked across at Penny and their gazes locked. Jake smiled gently at her and everyone clapped.

Penny swallowed the tears that had suddenly filled her eyes. Her father had always done that job and now another man had done so. Penny couldn't help thinking how much her father would have liked Jake and a warm, pleasant feeling burned in her chest. "Well," she said, clearing her throat, "everyone grab an ornament. The only rule is to try to space them out."

She was cheered when all the men got up and chose an ornament. It was almost as if they really wanted to decorate the tree. There were a few fall-outs when Harriet brought in more nachos, but they returned to the task at hand after a moment or two. With so many workers, it wasn't long before all the ornaments were hung.

Then Penny passed around candy canes. "These aren't your dinner! They go on the tree," she teased them with a smile.

Once that was done, Penny plugged in the Christmas tree lights as Harriet switched off the overhead lights.

There was complete silence as they all stared at the magic of the Christmas tree. After several minutes, Penny said softly, "Thank you. You did a magnificent job."

Then Harriet turned on the light again and invited them to come fix their sandwiches. Penny saw some disappointment in some faces, but she knew they'd cheer up once they saw the hot roast beef. Harriet had made some potato salad to go with the beef sandwiches and they also could have some hot cheese dip and chips.

As they were serving themselves, Penny brought in the presents she'd wrapped for them and placed them under the tree. Harriet encouraged them to take their plates into the den to eat in front of the tree. The presents were the first thing they all noticed.

"Hey, look! Santa's already come to see Penny," one of them said as he sat down. "He's pretty fast."

Penny put a Christmas CD on and the seasonal music played softly in the background. Then she fixed her plate, too. As she sat with the men around the tree and listened to the Christmas music, Penny felt a contented happiness steal over her. Glancing up she saw Jake, watching her intently. Their eyes met, for just a moment, and Penny felt something special pass between them, almost as if Jake understood how important this evening had been to her.

After everyone had their fill, Penny got up and said, "You will all get a Christmas bonus before you leave, but I thought it might be fun to have a gift, too." She paused and glanced at Jake, hoping he was going to approve of her next idea. Without her realizing it, Jake's approval had grown important to her and she continued nervously.

"But I don't really know you all very well, so I bought eight different gifts for guys, and you all are going to play a gift exchange game."

"Us?" Jake asked in surprise.

"Yes, Jake, even you," she said with a smile that she tried to keep from wobbling. "Here's how we play the game. Each of you will draw a number from the bowl Harriet will pass around. Whoever draws the first number gets to pick out any gift he wants. After he opens it and shows it to everyone, number two picks a gift *or* instead of picking a gift, he can take number one's gift."

There was an uproar of protest.

"Yes. But he doesn't get to open a gift. If he takes number one's gift, number one opens another gift. And we continue to number eight. That's the best number to draw because he can see everyone's gift before he takes the last unwrapped package. Any questions?"

No one had any questions.

Harriet passed around the bowl, letting them draw their numbers. Then Penny called for number one to choose a gift.

Dusty had drawn number one. He took a package from under the tree and unwrapped it, taking out a nice pair of work gloves, rough leather lined with sheepskin.

"Damn! These are nice!" he exclaimed.

Jake coughed and looked at Dusty.

"Uh, sorry, Penny, but I thought these would be joke gifts."

"That's all right, Dusty. I'm glad you like them."

"Yeah, but I won't get to keep 'em. Some of these guys are going to take them!"

"You never know." Penny sent him a sympathetic smile. When she glanced at Jake, she discovered he was smiling back at her. Clearly he thought the game had been a good idea and it pleased Penny enormously. When the next gift was opened, it was a leather vest. It and the gloves were soon stripped from their owners. But every gift seemed to please. The cowboys were torn between a new gift or those they could already see. The game was long and loud as protests rang out as someone lost his gift.

Penny and Harriet were as entertained as the players of the game. Finally Jake was the last to go, having drawn number eight and he took great pleasure in tormenting each of the men in taking their gifts. When it was over, Harriet jumped up to put out the desserts. Penny fixed the coffeepot and hoped it brewed quickly. She checked to make sure she had their bonuses ready in envelopes. She stacked them by the back door. They were all the same except for Jake's. His was on bottom.

The men's eyes grew large when they saw their dessert choices. In addition to cake or pie, they were each given an iced brownie, and they were all encouraged to have seconds of any of it. Penny served them coffee after they were seated.

One of the cowboys told an amusing story

about a Christmas past that reminded him of the evening. Another one told of a Christmas that had been terrible. Penny let her gaze drift to Jake, wondering about his Christmases. He caught her looking at him and smiled, but he didn't offer a story.

Most of the stories were amusing, but some were touching. The men lingered long after their plates were empty, though Harriet kept encouraging them to have seconds.

When they finally got up to go, Harriet stood by the door with the plate of brownies and offered a treat for the walk home.

Penny thanked them all for a delightful evening and handed them each an envelope. Only when Jake reached the door did she falter with her smile. But she managed a credible one, she thought, as she handed him an envelope.

He frowned. "I don't think I should get a bonus. I haven't been here long enough."

"You get Gerald's bonus. He didn't earn it."

"Penny, I don't—"

"I insist. It's Christmas."

"But I have my gift."

"That's from Santa. The bonus is from me."

"All right. Good night—and Merry Christmas."

"Merry Christmas and Jake—thank you."

Penny closed the door behind him. Leaning against the door, she looked at Harriet, cleaning up the dishes.

"That was a wonderful evening, wasn't it, Harriet?"

"Absolutely the best evening. It made Christmas in my heart."

"What a nice way to say it, Harriet. I hope you didn't mind that you didn't have a present under the tree. You'll have one before Christmas. I promise."

"I don't mind, Penny, really."

"Well, after your wonderful food tonight you'll also be getting a big bonus, too, especially if I can ask you to help me with another little Christmas surprise? For the Christmas party we are going to have to bake Christmas cookies that we package up for Santa to give to each child. Those have to be decorated. Then we bake regular cookies for everyone to enjoy. Do you think you could help me out?"

"Of course. I'll bake the Christmas cookies first. Then if we run short of time, you can decorate while I make more cookies. I've never been to the party, but it sounds nice."

"It is. Our parents started it when I was three and wanted to see Santa. They thought it would be better than driving all the way into Denver to find someone in a Santa suit. It's been going ever since."

"Who is the Santa?"

"We have—" She gulped. "Oh, dear. Dad and Uncle Bob used to take turns. We have two Santa suits. I'll go call Sally. Maybe she's made arrangements."

Sally said she had one person already enlisted, but that they'd need someone else to do it part of the time.

"Who is doing it for you?" Penny asked.

"He's new to town, but he agreed to help out."

"Okay, I'll get someone from this end. Which one will go first?"

"Let yours go first. I'm not sure this guy will be very good with little ones."

"That's fine. The tree will be there tomorrow morning so you'll have a couple of days for decorating."

"Perfect. Thanks, Penny."

"Oh, and Sally, the guys loved the presents you selected. We had a wonderful time."

"I'm glad."

"I wish you could've been here."

"Me, too, but we're really busy right now."

"Okay. I'll see you Saturday and Merry Christmas."

Penny hung up the phone and reached for her ski jacket. "Harriet, I'll be back to help in just a minute."

Harriet didn't seem upset and Penny scooted out the door.

When she reached the bunkhouse, she knocked on the door and waited.

When Jake opened the door, she said, "Hi, Jake, can I ask another favor of you?"

CHAPTER SEVEN

"Sure, Penny."

"Will you be Santa Claus on Saturday night at the town Christmas party?"

"What! Me? I've never played Santa Claus before."

"It's very easy. You do like little kids, don't you?"

"Well, yeah, but I haven't been around a lot of kids."

"That's all right. Just keep your voice gentle. You'll be relieved halfway through."

"Couldn't you ask the guy who played Santa last year?" As soon as the words left his mouth, Jake knew that it would be impossible for Penny to do so. The look in her eyes told him that this was another thing her dad used to do and he felt a sudden stab to the heart for being so insensitive.

"Dad and Uncle Bob used to do it, Jake. I wouldn't normally ask you to do this kind of thing, but Sally has already found one person, someone new to town, and I don't want to let everyone down."

Jake folded his arms and leaned back against the wall of the bunkhouse. "Uh, I don't have a Santa suit."

Penny's face lit up. "I have Dad's and he was almost as tall as you and we can stuff you with pillows to plump you up a bit. You can dress at Sally's store. Then when you finish your turn, you go back to the store and change clothes and come back to the party."

Jake took a deep breath, knowing what his answer was going to be, but not liking one bit the hold this young woman was beginning to have over him. "Okay, I'll be glad to participate."

"Oh, Jake, thank you so much, I really appreciate it." And he watched as she ran off back to the house.

Jake came back into the bunkhouse. The men were all still up, admiring their gifts and talking about their bonuses.

"Hey, Jake," Cookie asked, "Did you get a bonus?"

"Yeah, she insisted."

"Well, she was more generous this year than her dad ever was."

"Maybe that's because no one's going to skim money off the top this year. You didn't realize Gerald was cheating all of you, too, did you?"

"No, we hadn't thought of that," Dusty said. "We didn't approve of what he did, hell, we were hardly aware of it until he told us that night. But we sure didn't realize that was why the bonuses were so low."

"I'm guessing he took most of the spare money, and would've taken more if he'd thought he could get away with it. I'm glad she found out."

"But we don't know how she found out. Is she that good with numbers?" Dusty asked.

"I believe she overheard him telling all of you. She'd come down to tell him something and ran back to the house. Then she called the sheriff and told Gerald if he ever showed his face again, she'd file charges against him."

"Good for her. She sure is sweet and pretty, and out on her own. It's not fair."

"No, it's not," Jake agreed, thinking just how sweet and pretty Penny had looked when he'd agreed to be Santa. "But we all know life's not fair. If it were, we'd all be rich and owning our own spreads, right?"

They all laughed.

"Hey, what did Penny come down here for? Did we forget something we should'a done?" Cookie asked.

"No, I guess I can tell all of you since I don't expect you to sit on my lap Saturday night. I'm playing Santa for half of the party."

There was silence for a moment as all the men looked at Jake and then at each other. "Whew," Dusty said finally. "That's a relief. I wondered where you were going with that lap comment."

Everyone laughed at Dusty's teasing Jake. They'd all been a little worried since Jake seemed so stern sometimes. But they were beginning to warm up to him.

Jake told them all good-night and took his gift and bonus with him to his room. He'd had the last number in the gift exchange game and after a lot of teasing had eventually chosen the least popular gift.

After he put the gift away, he sat down at his

desk and opened the envelope holding the bonus. He pulled out five one-hundred-dollar bills. He knew how much the men had gotten since he'd seen Cookie open his envelope and count the money. They'd each received two hundred and fifty dollars.

She'd doubled their amount for him? He hadn't been here very long. Penny was demonstrating a lot of confidence in him. He hoped he lived up to it.

Taking out his lock box, he put the money inside. Then he locked it and put it on the bottom shelf and covered it with some books. He didn't have any qualms about the men bothering with it. But bunkhouses had been broken into before. Not often, of course, because they didn't think cowboys had anything worth stealing, except their horses.

With a sigh, he dressed for bed and got under the covers, after turning off the light. He closed his eyes and saw Penny standing in front of the Christmas tree, explaining the gift exchange game. He hadn't seen any pain in her eyes for the first time since he'd met her. She'd looked beautiful, her dark hair shiny and· long, her cheeks flushed.

He groaned and shifted in his bed. He needed to get Penny out of his head. A new thought replaced that one. He saw her when she was asking him to play Santa. She'd smiled eagerly at him because she wanted a favor from him. Of course, it wasn't for her, and it hadn't been a very big one, but it had been a favor, nonetheless.

Maybe he should keep that look in his mind. She could look damned appealing when she wanted something. Too appealing. No, he couldn't keep that thought in his mind. He'd give her anything when she looked at him like that.

It made him think of Dexter's wife. She'd looked at him that way, and he hadn't been interested. In fact, he'd thought she looked revolting when she tried to get him to give her what she wanted. Of course, it hadn't been anything innocent, like playing Santa Claus. He tried to imagine Penny asking him to sleep with her. Damn! He'd start removing his clothes before she finished asking!

Where had that thought come from? Penny wouldn't ask him to do that. She was too—too innocent. At least he thought she was. Maybe she had a boyfriend in town. He'd have to ask someone. Who would know?

The only person who would really know was her cousin in town. What was her name? Sally, that was it. He could ask Sally, but then she might tell Penny and he'd be embarrassed.

He shifted in his bed again and forced his eyes shut, trying to rid himself of images of Penny before he went out of his mind.

Penny called the bunkhouse the next morning to tell Jake she would be working with Harriet for the next two days to prepare all the cookies for the Christmas party. She'd go back to work on Monday.

After she hung up the phone, she sat down to the breakfast Harriet had prepared for her. Harriet joined her at the table, having cooked her own breakfast, too. "What did Jake say?"

"He said that would be fine. What else could he say? I'm the boss."

Harriet just ate her eggs, toast and bacon, not saying anything.

"Right?" Penny asked insistently.

"Right," Harriet agreed.

"He didn't sound angry."

"And I suppose a day or two off won't matter in the grand scheme of things," Harriet added.

"That's right," Penny agreed with relief. "I'm sure that's what he thought, too."

"Does anyone ever make brownies or candy?" Harriet asked, changing the subject.

"For the party, you mean? I don't think so, but I don't see why not. Would you like to make some of those things?"

"Well, the brownies were popular last night. I could make some more batches of those. Doing the icing is easy."

"I think that's a good idea. There's only one other lady who does the baking that I know of."

"Okay, well, let her know what we're bringing if you need to. I'll keep thinking up things to fix." Harriet carried her now empty plate over to the sink. After she put them away, she started getting down mixing bowls. "But I'm still doing the sugar cookies first so you can get started on decorating them. They'll be cool by ten o'clock."

"Yes, ma'am," Penny said, as if she were reporting to duty. "I'll go vacuum the den from last night. Though I thought they were very neat in their eating habits." She grinned so Harriet would know she was teasing.

"Not bad for a bunch of cowboys, were they?" Harriet teased back.

Penny laughed and went to get out the vacuum cleaner. She spent the next half hour straightening the den. Then she plugged in the tree lights and stared at their beautiful tree. It looked the same as it had every other year. Everything around it had changed, but it remained the same.

She missed her parents so much. But they were there with her, in a way. She felt their love. Her mother had always said they would be with her, even if they died. Since she'd lost her son, she talked about death occasionally. Penny found comfort in those words now.

"I feel you, Mom," she whispered, tears filling her eyes.

A warmth filled her that surprised her. Maybe it was just the thought of her mother, or maybe it was really her spirit, but Penny felt comforted.

Finally she turned off the tree lights and left the den.

She went upstairs and cleaned her room followed by the bathroom. Then she went downstairs to help Harriet with the cookies.

"Okay, all my jobs are done so now, I'm going to mix the icing for painting the cookies."

"Do you do it from scratch?"

"Yes. Mom has—had a recipe that spreads really well. It's butter icing."

"I've never found a good one. Do you mind if I copy it?"

"Of course not. Mom had to figure it out because sometimes the bought icing was very expensive."

Penny began taking out the ingredients she needed. She melted some ingredients on the stove. While that was happening, she put the dry ingredients into a mixing bowl. Then she combined them and beat it with the mixer. When she was finished she had a big bowl of white icing. She then took down four bowls and filled each with icing. She covered the rest of the icing with plastic wrap and put it away.

Next, she took out food coloring and mixed each bowl with a different color. When that was done, she set the four bowls over on the breakfast table and put four spreading knives down on the table, too. "I'm ready. Are those first cookies cool enough?"

Harriet leaned over and felt of them. "I

believe so. It's the cutting out that takes so long, isn't it?"

"I'm afraid so. That's why the rest of the cookies aren't sugar cookies. Only Santa's cookies are decorated."

"That was a wise decision," Harriet said with a smile.

"It was my mother's. After the first Christmas, she vowed never to decorate another cookie. She did, of course, but not nearly as many."

Penny got busy decorating. It was slow work, since she wanted each cookie to be beautiful. Harriet delivered several more batches before lunch. By the time Harriet had lunch ready, left over beef sandwiches with potato salad, Penny had done half the baked cookies.

"My, you're doing a fine job," Harriet said.

"Thanks. Like you said, though, it's slow work."

"You're going faster than I thought you would."

"Well, I'm ready for lunch. I love these sandwiches."

"They did turn out well. And we didn't have as many left over as I thought we would."

As they sat and ate their lunch Penny remembered one more thing she needed to do for the Saturday night party, but she'd do it later. They both enjoyed their sandwiches and cleaned up after it.

Then it was back to decorating cookies for Penny. Harriet baked four batches of brownies for a change of pace.

By dinnertime, Penny's back was aching and she hated the sight of bare sugar cookies. She stretched as she called it quits for the day. "Tomorrow we'll need more sugar cookies, but no more tonight, Harriet."

"I agree. Did you use all the icing?"

"No, I still have plenty mixed up. I'll put the big bowl in the fridge, but I may have to warm it up in the microwave in the morning."

"So we need to bag these cookies, the ones you've decorated?"

"Yes. Put four cookies in each bag and try not to get two alike."

They both bagged cookies for half an hour. They had seventy-nine bags.

"Will we have more kids than that?" Harriet asked in amazement.

"Yes. They come from all over. Word has spread that it's free, you see. Once we talked about cutting back, but Mom talked to a lady that year who told her this was the only bit of Christmas her kids would get because the year had been so bad. That just broke Mom's heart, and she never suggested we cut back again."

"No, I can see how she'd feel that way. It gives me more energy to make those sugar cookies tomorrow, too."

"Yeah. We put out a collection box for those who want to help out, and that money goes to help families who wouldn't have a good Christmas after all."

"Your parents' clothes are going to be put out on racks in a discreet area, along with Sally's folks' things, in case someone wants to take them home and wrap them up for family members, too. Sally told me someone would monitor it so no one would get greedy and take everything."

"Oh, good. That makes me feel good. Mom would like her things helping someone at Christmas time."

"Well, I have to say that's a really nice thing to do. Your parents both sound like extraordinary people, Penny."

"Yes. They both loved Christmas. And I do, too."

"What's not to like?" Harriet asked with a laugh.

"I couldn't agree more."

The next afternoon, Jake knocked on the back door, wanting to ask what time he should be in town to put on the Santa uniform.

Penny answered as she sucked on a finger. "Hi, Jake."

"Did you cut your finger?" he asked, instantly worried.

"No, I was licking off icing so I wouldn't get it on the door handle."

"Licking off icing?"

He looked a little confused, so Penny explained that she was icing cookies.

"I haven't done that in years," he said, and Penny immediately pulled him inside.

"I need help. Come wash your hands." She led him to the kitchen sink where she washed hers and then moved aside for him to wash his.

"But I have work I need to do."

"Yes, you do. Decorating cookies. I got started late and have about fifty more to do. I need help…it's for the children, Jake."

The pleading look in her eyes reminded him

of his dreams the night before. As he suspected, he couldn't turn her down. "Okay, but I'm not sure I'm any good at this."

When he got to the table and saw her handiwork, he started backing away.

"Jake, where are you going?" she demanded.

"I'm not an artist, like you are."

"You can do the easy parts. Look, you can paint the bells red and I'll put some decoration on them. Then you paint the suit on the Santa Claus cookie and I'll paint his face and beard. See? It will be easy."

He finally sat down at the table and she showed him what she wanted him to do. After a few minutes he was moving through the cookies quickly.

"Why isn't Harriet helping you?" he eventually thought to ask.

"She's upstairs going through my parents' belongings to see if there is anything that might be in good enough shape to offer as presents for any needy families. People bring items each year that others might like. I think it will be a good thing to do with my parents' things."

Jake cleared his throat. "That's very generous of you, Penny."

"Not that generous. I took out a few things that I wanted to keep. But it's what my parents would have wanted. I know they would be happy about it. So I am, too."

"Bailey is a nice town, but I had no idea Christmas was so special here. You all go to an awful lot of trouble."

"A lot of people come a long way for our Christmas party. You're going to get tired of lifting kids to your knee tomorrow night."

"Any big girls come to sit on Santa's lap?"

Penny grinned at him, noting the teasing look on his face. "More than you think, but they don't get cookies unless they are preteen or less."

His smile disappeared and he looked alarmed. "You're kidding!"

"No, I'm not. Especially when they see you without your Santa garb on, so keep the beard in place until you're inside the store."

"I will."

"Dad always said the beard was the worst part of the costume."

"Hmm, I hadn't thought of that." He scratched his chin. "I grew my beard out once when I was working up in the mountains for the winter. At least I grew it as long as I could stand it. I finally shaved it off about halfway through."

Penny looked at him thoughtfully, "I can't imagine you with a beard."

"It wasn't pretty. I finally figured out a beard takes almost as much work as shaving every morning. The men in pictures with beards must've had themselves trimmed by a barber. They didn't look too natural."

"The same goes for the ladies."

Jake looked startled. "You mean they—oh, you mean they get prettied up by someone."

"Definitely."

"I think you'd look good in a magazine without too much work."

Penny blushed. "No, no, I wouldn't."

They sat together in silence for a little while longer. It had been nice talking to Jake, his comment about her looking good had embarrassed her a little, but a warm feeling had settled in her stomach when she thought that Jake found her attractive.

Not wanting to break the mood, Penny asked softly, "Did you finish putting the red on the Santas?"

"I've got a couple more to do."

They worked quietly for a while longer.

Finally Penny asked, "What did you come to the house for? I forgot to ask you."

"I wanted to know how early I'll need to be in town to get dressed in the Santa costume. When does the party start?"

"It starts at five. You'd better get there by four-thirty. I'll help you get dressed."

He looked shocked.

"Don't worry Jake, you just pull it on over your clothes. Do you have black boots?"

"Cowboy boots," he said with a shrug.

"Perfect. What else would Santa wear?"

They grinned in unison at those words.

"What time are you going?"

"Same as you. We have to get the cookies and other desserts in place. Harriet will take care of that once I introduce her to some of the ladies who will work those tables tomorrow night."

"Then why don't you both ride with me? There's no need to take both vehicles."

CHAPTER EIGHT

LATER that afternoon Jake and Penny were still decorating cookies when Harriet came back into the kitchen carrying several boxes with her. "Okay, I think I've sorted nearly everything out that can go to the party. There are just the things your mom bought your dad. Have you decided what you want to do with them yet, Penny?"

"Yes, I think so. I know they're expensive, but I can't use them so I think they should go to the needy families, too. My parents would appreciate someone getting use out of them. Unless, Jake wanted the boots. What size do you wear?"

"Elevens," Jake said, looking at the boxes.

"That's what these are, Jake, and they are mighty fine," Harriet assured him, taking off the lid.

"Yeah, I guess they are," he said, picking them up and looking at them. "How about I pay for them, Penny? If you don't want to keep the money, you can put it in the pot tomorrow night."

"You can just have them, Jake."

"No, I need to pay for them. What did they cost?"

"I'm not taking money for them, Jake. You can make a donation to the pot tomorrow if you like, that will be enough."

"These are fine boots, Penny. I recognize the name on the box. All those kind of boots cost a lot of money, at least two hundred and fifty dollars."

"Ok, you can donate fifty dollars—that seems like a fair price to me." She didn't intend to waver.

He studied her for a minute, but her stubbornness was shown in her raised chin.

"Okay. Fifty dollars." He drew out his billfold and counted out the money. Then he said, "Thanks, Penny."

"Don't you want to try them on?"

"Okay." He removed his work boots and pulled the new boots on. "They're a perfect fit.

And look, they're black. I can wear them tomorrow night."

Penny sighed. "You might as well take the other box, too, Jake. They're both part of the deal."

"What's in the other box?"

"Something no one will want. I mean, it's nice, and my dad would've enjoyed them, wearing them to church, but they couldn't be worn to work. They'd fall apart. I'd like you to have them."

Curious now, Jake reached for the other box. Inside he found the cashmere scarf and gloves. "Whoa, these feel great. I'll pay fifty dollars for these, too. I don't have it on me, but tomorrow—"

"No. I won't take any more money. Accept them as my gift to you. This money is already a lot to go in the pot tomorrow night. It will help a lot of people."

"But what about these other boxes?" Harriet asked. "I found them in your dad's things. I guess he got them for your mom or you, but there are no labels on them."

Penny stared at the boxes, not moving.

"Penny? Aren't you going to open them?"

She drew a tear-laden breath. "I can't."

Jake knelt down beside her, wanting to take away her pain. "Sure you can, honey. Me and Harriet are both here with you."

Penny looked into Jake's steady gaze and knew that he was right. She needed to do this and she could do it with him beside her. Slowly she took the first package from Harriet and opened it. She knew immediately it was a gift for her. She'd pointed out a bracelet similar to it once when she and her father had gone to Denver. Tears began streaming down her face and Jake wrapped a strong protective arm around her. Without a word, she buried her face on his shoulder.

"What's wrong, Penny? What is it?"

"I—I showed Daddy some bracelets like that once. I was just teasing, but he must've gone back and—" The tears were coming so fast she couldn't talk anymore.

"Harriet, I think you'd better get us some tissues," Jake suggested.

She reappeared quickly. "Here you go, honey. Sit up and wipe your face before you get Jake's shirt all wet."

That immediately made Penny smile as she

realized that she'd been crying on Jake's shoulder. "I-I'm so s-sorry, Jake."

"It's not a problem, Penny. Do you think you are ready to open the other box now?"

She nodded and took the other box. It was smaller than the last and Jake hoped it wouldn't have the same effect on Penny. But it was even worse. Penny cried even more tears this time, burying her face in her hands as she sobbed.

The gift was a set of wedding rings. Jake and Harriet looked at each other, but they didn't understand the significance.

"Dad always teased Mom," Penny said when she finally wiped up her tears. "When they got married, he couldn't afford any diamonds. She just wore a plain band. This year he bought her diamonds."

Fresh tears rolled down her cheeks as she finished talking and Jake mopped them up. "You should keep these rings. You can use them when you get married."

"Yes," she said, sniffing. "I guess so. I'd like that."

Harriet put the bangle bracelet on Penny's wrist. "Now you'll always have a memory of your dad's love. Just like the presents from your mom."

"Yes." She looked up briefly at both Jake and Harriet. "I'm sorry for all the tears."

"Understandable. And if you sit on my lap Saturday night, I'll wave the cookie rule just for you."

"Jake!" Penny exclaimed, shocked by his words, but pleased that he had lightened the mood. He had a real knack for making her feel better.

"Aw, I was just teasing, honey," he said, not realizing he had used that word again.

Penny's cheeks turned a bright red.

Harriet laughed. "Looks like you're both red-faced."

"Maybe it's time for me to leave," Jake said, keeping his gaze on Penny.

"Hey! We still have some cookies to finish. You aren't going to have me do it on my own are you?"

"Okay, but we'd better get busy." Jake sat back down beside Penny, looking at her.

"Right."

Harriet excused herself to do a few chores and just Jake and Penny worked on the

Christmas cookies, with Christmas music playing in the background.

Jake couldn't help watching Penny as she carefully decorated each cookie. She showed her care for the children with each careful stroke. He loved that about her.

She suddenly looked up and caught him staring at her. "Don't you have cookies to decorate?"

"Sure, but—but I enjoy watching you," he said, smiling at her.

Her cheeks turned red. "I'm just decorating the cookies."

"I know, but you put so much effort into it."

"I want the children to like what they get."

"I imagine they will. But I didn't know the job was so big. Do people know how hard you work to pull off the festival?"

"I'm sure they do. But I enjoy it. It makes me feel a part of the community, a part of Christmas."

"I think you should be the Santa Claus."

Penny smiled at his teasing. "Oh, no, Jake, I think you'll be a much better Santa."

"Hmm, I guess I have the natural qualifications for the job, but you have the heart. I've never known such a generous person as you."

"I'm just filled with the Christmas spirit. That's all."

"No, not really." He grinned and leaned over and kissed her briefly. "But maybe I am."

Penny was taken by total surprise and didn't know how to react. She'd liked the feel of his kiss, but she wasn't supposed to mix romance with business, was she?

"Jake, I— We—" Penny struggled for something to say to explain how she was feeling, but Jake interrupted her by putting his long finger over her mouth.

"You don't have to say anything, let's just put it down to festive cheer. Let's get back to these cookies or we'll never get them done in time!"

When they finished, it was suppertime and Harriet came in, insisting Jake should stay and eat with them. "You've done good work. You deserve a good meal."

Penny relieved Jake's mind. "It's all right, Jake. She put a meat loaf in the oven before she went upstairs. Can't you smell it? You deserve a reward for all your help this afternoon."

"I'll stay, especially if Harriet's cooking."

"He's something, isn't he?" Harriet said with a smile.

"He's a very nice person," Penny said sedately.

Jake smiled and looked at Penny, "Thank you, ma'am. I do my best."

"Dinner's ready," Harriet announced with a smile. "Penny made the salad."

"That didn't take a lot of cooking," Penny protested.

"No, but you make a good salad. Mine always get too soggy."

They all sat down at the table and Harriet offered a prayer. Then everyone dug in, Jake filling his plate.

"It's so good to look at something other than sugar cookies. I'd still be decorating if you hadn't helped me, Jake," Penny said.

"It was worth it for the price of this dinner."

"We're glad you're eating with us," Harriet assured him. "I must say it's nice to cook something other than cookies!"

He suddenly frowned. "Did you bake all of the cookies, Harriet?"

"You didn't realize that before now, Jake?" Penny asked.

"No, some slave driver kept me working on sugar cookies all day," he said, grinning at her.

"Oh, you!" Penny beamed at Harriet.

"Harriet has baked for two straight days after our Christmas decorating party."

"Harriet, I think you deserve an award. Do you want to sit on Santa's knee?"

"Watch it, young man, or I'll line up every grandma in the county to sit on your lap." Jake looked worried for a moment but then saw that she was grinning and started to laugh, too.

"Yes, ma'am. I'll behave."

Penny was smiling as she ate her dinner.

Jake watched her before he asked what he wanted to know. "Why are you smiling, Penny?"

She stared at her plate. Then she looked at him. "It was just nice, hearing you both laughing at the table. Mom and Dad used to tease each other a lot."

"That's a nice memory to have," he said softly.

"Yes, I have a lot of good memories. They were great parents. I miss them a lot."

The table fell silent for a moment and then Jake stood and took his leave. Penny and Harriet both promised to be ready the next day at four-thirty for the drive into Bailey.

Together, she and Harriet cleaned the dishes

and each vowed to have an early night. Penny went upstairs to her bedroom, but she wasn't really tired. Her mind kept wandering back to the kiss she had shared with Jake and the wonderful relaxed meal they had all enjoyed together. Even though her parents were gone she felt as though she was going to enjoy this Christmas after all. She found a favorite book on her bookshelf and settled down to read. A few minutes later, the telephone interrupted her.

"Hello?"

"Penny, it's Sally. I'm sorry to disturb you, but do you have something red to wear tomorrow night?"

"Red? Why would I wear red?"

"Because you're going to have to be Santa's helper. My guy says he can't do it if he doesn't have a helper and we need to keep things the same for each Santa."

"We've never had a Santa's helper before."

"I know, but our dads didn't need to be helped. They were experienced with kids. My guy says he can't do it if he doesn't have a helper. Will you wear something red?"

"All right. I guess so. I have a heavy sweater

I can wear without a coat over it. But I don't have red pants. I'll have to wear black pants."

"Okay, I can do that, too. It will be close enough. What time will you be here by?"

"We were going to leave here at four-thirty. So we shouldn't be too long after that. We can try to leave a little earlier, about ten after four? That should give us a little leeway."

"Good. The tree looks wonderful by the way, it's really perfect, Penny. I can't wait until we turn the lights on tomorrow night. I'll see you then."

"I'm glad you like the tree, it took some finding. Bye."

Penny hung up the phone. Then she picked it back up to tell Jake about the change of time tomorrow night. When the phone was answered Penny asked to speak to Jake and waited for him to come to the phone, then she said, "Jake, it's Penny. I just talked to my cousin and she'd like us to be there a little earlier, at least by four-thirty. Can you be ready then?"

"Sure, as long as you'll be done with your cookies by then."

Penny started to laugh, "Yes, I'm sure we'll

be done by then. Oh and by the way, you're going to have a little help tomorrow night. Sally said her volunteer wouldn't be Santa unless he had a helper."

"So Sally's going to help both of us out?" Jake asked.

"No. Sally will help her Santa and I'm going to be helping you."

"Well, I have to say I like the sound of that. I'll see you tomorrow afternoon."

"Yes, good night, Jake."

The next day, Harriet got an early start on the baking. When Penny came downstairs, she found her housekeeper taking a cookie sheet out of the oven already.

"Oh, my, you got up early, Harriet."

"Good morning. Yes, I did. I don't like to leave things to the last minute."

"By the way I'm going to be Santa's helper while Jake is Santa. It seems Sally's volunteer refused to play Santa if she didn't stay with him."

"Hmm, that sounds interesting," Harriet said with a small smile playing on her lips.

"Oh, I'm sure it's just because he's inexperienced."

"Jake didn't ask that you help him, did he?"

"No, but Sally thinks it would be too noticeable for one Santa to have help and not the other one."

"That's a good point and it should make the evening fun for both of you. Just a minute and I'll have your breakfast ready."

After breakfast they both got busy with some final preparations and didn't stop until it was almost three-thirty. When Jake knocked on their back door at ten after four, both ladies were dressed and ready. They carried out six boxes of cookies and left the other boxes for Jake.

As she walked by him, Penny realized that Jake was wearing the present he had got at the tree decorating party—a dark blue shirt and tie. Penny had to admit he looked very nice. He was wearing a nice coat, too, and she thought how different he looked from his normal cowboy attire. For a moment she wanted to comment on his appearance, but she was afraid he'd think she was flirting with him.

Harriet, however, didn't hesitate. "Boy, you look really nice, Jake. You got some girl in town you want to impress?"

"I just thought I should dress up for the party. Penny said it was a real special occasion." Jake looked slightly uncomfortable for a moment.

"You do look nice, Jake," Penny finally said with a little smile.

"Thank you, Penny. You look real nice, too."

They looked at each other for a brief moment and then Jake went back in to the house to get the rest of their things. Finally they were in the truck and on their way.

"When we get there, I'll carry the cookie boxes marked with an S to the Santa chair. Then we'll need to hurry to get to the general store to change," Penny explained.

"Okay, General," Jake said with a teasing grin.

Penny blushed. "Well, I thought I should explain what needs to happen when we get there."

"I was just teasing. You're right. We're going to be on a tight schedule, I guess. I play Santa from five until six-thirty?"

"That's right. Then we'll put up the sign saying Santa is taking a little break. We'll go to the general store and the other Santa and Sally will come out and take our places."

"Will we really need a break?" Jake asked.

"You'll want one after lifting all those children onto your lap. Wait until you hear some of them screaming the entire time with the parents taking pictures. You'll wear out fast," Harriet joked.

"They cry?" Jake asked, startled.

"Not for very long, Jake. It won't be that bad."

"You may have to start lining up your volunteers for next year, Penny, if it's very bad," Jake said. "I didn't plan on them crying."

"They're little kids and you're a stranger, no matter what their parents say. Just stay calm and everything will be okay. Oh! I haven't thought of a name for you to call me. What would Santa's helper be named?"

"How about Rudolph?" Harriet suggested with a giggle.

"I think it will be obvious that I'm a female," Penny said.

"Yeah, I think it will," Jake said with a sideways look at Penny.

Her cheeks turned red as Penny stared straight ahead.

"That's it!" Jake said, grinning. "I'll call you Rosy. How's that for a fake name?"

"I was hoping for something more exotic," Penny said, a little disgruntled.

"I might not be able to remember something exotic, but it will be easy to remember Rosy. All I'll have to do is look at your rosy cheeks."

Penny could feel her cheeks heating up again and said nothing.

Harriet chuckled. "I think you have a point, Jake. Rosy it is."

Sally's volunteer wasn't there when they arrived, so Penny and Jake didn't get to meet him. Jake put on his Santa costume and Sally helped him with his beard, using theatrical glue to make it stick to his face.

Even Penny wasn't sure she would recognize him if she didn't know it was Jake under the fluffy white beard and the rounded figure.

"Okay, Jake, say ho, ho, ho," Penny directed him.

"Ho, ho, ho," Jake said in his deep voice.

"My, he has the voice for it, doesn't he?" Sally asked.

"Yes, he does."

"Are we ready, Rosy?" Jake asked. Penny was wearing a heavy red sweater over her black pants.

"Wait, Penny," Sally said. "You have to wear a Santa hat. Here it is." She pinned it on to Penny's head.

"Okay, thanks, Sally. We'll be back at six-thirty."

"Have fun."

Jake took a minute to admire her hat. "Is that a sprig of mistletoe on your cap?"

Suddenly nervous, Penny felt clumsily for the sprig on her hat. "Oh, no, I'm sure it's a fake sprig of holly."

Jake stepped a little closer to Penny, his voice suddenly very deep and quiet. "I think it's mistletoe, which means I need to kiss you before I go outside and have to be Santa." And before Penny could argue he did exactly that. His lips were warm and persuasive on hers and for a brief moment Penny relaxed into the kiss. She had to admit, Jake was a very good kisser. Then, reluctantly, Jake ended the kiss and stood smiling down into Penny's big blue eyes.

Penny stared at him in shock, and he laughed and kissed her quickly again. "Now, I can be Santa."

Penny took a deep breath and only hoped

she could be his helper. Right now, she wasn't sure she could keep her mind on the job.

They walked outside. In the half hour since their arrival, the town and its visitors had filled in the town circle around the big tree that Jake and his men had cut down days before.

"We'll turn the lights on at six. As Santa you'll throw the switch, or push the button or whatever. Mr. Robinson rigged the lights up so he'll be there to show you what to do. You'll be glad to stretch your legs at that point."

"Is that a line of kids already waiting for me?"

"Yes, Santa, it certainly is. Isn't it nice to know you're so popular?"

"I think you may owe me for this," he growled under his breath and again Penny felt a warm sensation. She had to keep her mind focused, but it was hard when she had to be so near to Jake!

Then, like a natural, he waved to the kids, calling out, "Merry Christmas!"

He got a mixed reaction. Many people responded with Merry Christmas. Others, mostly little children, cried. The older kids jumped up and down shouting all kinds of things.

Jake stepped up on the small platform and sat down in the large wooden chair. "Well, now, who is here to see me? Come right up, little boy."

The first in line was a chubby little boy about two years old. His parents pushed him forward.

"What's your name?" Santa asked.

"Wobert," the child wobbled.

"Well, Robert, what do you want Santa to bring you?"

"A horsey."

Jake sent a worried look to Penny.

Penny leaned forward. "Do you mean a real horse or a play horse, Robert?"

"A play horsey," Robert responded.

"Oh," Jake said with relief. "Well, I'll see what I can do, Robert. Rosy, do you have some special cookies for Robert?"

"Yes, I do. Here you go, Robert. Merry Christmas."

Jake leaned near Penny. "One down, a thousand to go."

After twenty or so kids, Penny thought things were going well, until Jake leaned closer and said, "Er, Rosy…I think we had an accident."

CHAPTER NINE

PENNY looked down to see a very nervous little girl sitting quietly in Jake's lap. Nerves had clearly got the better of her and she was looking very sheepish indeed. Instead of saying anything to embarrass the little girl further, Penny simply lifted her off Jake's lap and handed her back to her mom. Then she stepped forward and said, "Santa is going to take a little break now and go and turn on the Christmas tree lights. Then he'll be back to see you."

She stepped back to take Santa's arm, whispering, "Your costume is very thick. It won't get to your clothes and it may dry out while you're turning on the tree lights."

"Okay. Where do I go?"

"That's Mr. Robinson at the bottom of the stairs. He'll guide you to the switch. I'm going to go stand in front of the tree so I can see how pretty it looks."

Jake stepped down and shook Mr. Robinson's hand. Then the pair walked around the tree to the back. Penny hurried to stand with the crowd surrounding the big tree. It was completely dark by then, but there were floodlights that provided lights for everyone.

Santa (aka Jake) announced that they were going to shut down the floodlights for a few minutes so the tree lights could be better seen, so everyone needed to stand still so there would be no accidents.

Penny grinned. Mr. Robinson had prompted Jake well. Suddenly the floodlights went out and there was a gasp from the audience. Then the Christmas tree lights came on and everyone cheered.

Penny breathed a sigh of relief. The tree looked wonderful and Penny was sure that her parents were both there with her to see it. It had been important for both her and Sally to fulfill the duties of their families this Christmas and they had done it. The festival was going well. She stepped around the tree to the tables where several ladies, including

Harriet, were providing cookies to one and all.

"Is everything going all right, Harriet?" Penny whispered.

"Oh, yes. I'm so glad I've been a part of this, Penny. It's the best Christmas I can ever remember."

"After all your hard work, I'm glad you're enjoying it."

"Yes. One man came to the table and asked how much the cookies were. I told him they were free and he brought two little children to the table and told them they could each have one. I gave them three, instead, and their eyes lit up. Since they weren't dressed very warmly, I told him about the free clothes and toys on the other side of the circle and they went over there. It felt so good to know that I was doing something to help people who needed it."

"Yes, that's the reason for the Christmas festival." Penny smiled and moved back toward Santa's chair. She knew Jake would return soon. But Harriet's story stayed with her. She knew her parents would've been pleased.

When Jake settled back down in his chair,

Penny leaned forward and asked, "Are you okay now? Did your pants dry out?"

"Yeah, you were right. Let's see if we can whittle down the line of kids before Santa number two gets here."

Penny stepped forward and motioned for the next child to come see Santa. The parents stepped forward with their camera, ready to take pictures.

Jake lifted the cutest little girl onto his lap. "Ho, ho, ho, what's your name?"

"Penny," the child said solemnly.

Jake sent his helper a quick look. Then he turned back to his customer. "Well, Penny, what do you want Santa to bring you this year?"

The little girl was probably three years old, but she spoke clearly. "I want a baby doll. Mommy said I should ask for a real baby, but I want a play baby."

Jake shot a look at the woman, obviously pregnant. "Well, Santa will do his best. Maybe you might even get both, if you're really good."

"Here are your special Santa cookies," the older Penny said, handing the child a packet of decorated cookies. The little girl took the cookies and slid down from Santa's lap.

Penny suspected the next two children might be the ones Harriet had told her about. They were poorly dressed, though clean and neat, and they didn't look like they had enough to eat. Jake took both of them on his lap and asked what they wanted for Christmas. They both looked rather frightened.

Penny looked at the mother standing down below. She stepped down and asked, "Have you looked at the toy table? I'm sure there are things there that the children might like."

"Oh, yes, thank you. It's been s-so wonderful. We got them each a new outfit and some toys."

"Could you use some money for food?" Penny asked.

The woman looked shocked. "Oh, no, we've taken so much already."

Penny took the fifty dollars Jake had given her from her pocket. She had intended to put it in the contribution jar, but she would just be skipping the middle man. "Please take this to help out. We want you to have a Merry Christmas."

The woman looked at Penny and tears of gratitude filled her eyes.

"Er, Rosy, do you have cookies for these two?" Jake asked, recalling Penny to her duties. She stepped up and presented each of the children with a bag of cookies. The threesome walked away in a daze. Penny knew she'd done the right thing, and it had felt good.

When six-thirty rolled around, Jake looked at Penny. "Time for a break?"

"Yes, Santa, I think so." She stepped forward. "Santa is going to take a short break. Then he'll come back and see the rest of you."

She took Santa's hand to lead him down from his chair. When they began the walk back to the General Store, Penny went to let go of Jake's hand, but he held on tight to hers. "Jake, someone will see us!"

"So Santa likes his helper. There's nothing wrong with that."

She told herself Jake was still role-playing. But she was beginning to worry that it might mean more than that to her. Her hand felt too good in his.

When they opened the door to the General Store, there were a lot of shoppers milling around, taking the opportunity of a trip to town to do some shopping.

Penny led Jake toward the back of the store, where Sally had let them dress earlier. Inside, they found another Santa just finishing attaching his beard.

"Hello, Santa," Penny said. "I don't believe we've met. I'm Penny, Sally's cousin and this Santa is Jake, my ranch manager."

"I'm Hunter. It's nice to meet you both. Is it my turn now?"

"You've got a few minutes," Jake said. "Where's your helper?"

Just then the door opened and Sally walked in. "I'm here. I just had to check on a couple of things. The store is exceptionally busy this evening."

"Yes. Do I need to help out in here?" Penny asked.

"No, I've got three workers, so they should be all right. Hunter, are you ready?"

"Lead the way, Sally," the man said in a deep voice.

"Good luck," Jake called out. Then he looked at Penny. "Can I take off the beard now? You were right about it. It's driving me crazy."

"Yes. Let me close the door, so no little children can see you come out of your costume." After she'd secured the door, she returned to Jake's side. "You know, I wouldn't be able to pick Hunter out in a crowd since we only saw him in costume."

"That's true," Jake said, tugging on his beard.

"No, wait, you're going to destroy it," she said and stepped closer so that she could detach the beard the proper way. Finally she had removed all the white fluff.

Jake scratched his skin. "Oh, this feels so good."

"Wait, I need to remove your eyebrows, too." She bent over him, carefully removing the eyebrows. Penny realized that she was standing rather close to Jake.

"All done." Penny said putting some much needed distance between them. Jake smiled at her as if he understood her nervousness and started unbuttoning his jacket and pants. Soon he was standing in front of her, looking like himself.

"I understand now why your dad and uncle took turns being Santa. Those kids were cute, but they wear you down after a while. Say, I meant to ask, what did you say to the lady with the two little kids who didn't look like they got much to eat?"

"I gave her the fifty dollars you'd given me. I was going to put it in the jar, but I decided they needed the money for food."

"Good job, Penny. You've got a big heart."

"The money didn't belong to me. And helping people is what the festival is all about. They'd gotten some toys and an outfit each from the other tables and Harriet told me that she gave them three cookies each."

"Then they'll have a Merry Christmas."

"Yes, I hope they do."

"Shall we go have a cookie or two ourselves, now? I think Mr. Robinson said the choir was going to sing about now, too."

"Yes. That's the high school choir. They're very good," Penny said with pride.

Penny had pulled off the red sweater, leaving her in a white blouse. She put on her coat and joined Jake as they walked through the store. Outside, he caught her hand again and headed toward the Christmas tree still looking beautiful lit up with its lights and the floodlights. There was still a large crowd around it, no one wanting to leave early.

The choir started singing Christmas carols and Jake and Penny stopped by the dessert table and each got an oatmeal-raisin cookie to keep them going. After all, they'd had to eat dinner at four. Penny drifted closer to the tree, admiring it, thinking Jake was right behind her.

Suddenly she realized he wasn't and turned back, only to see him coming toward her. "I wondered what had happened to you."

"I was talking to Harriet. She's really enjoying herself."

"Yes, I think it's wonderful."

"It's all thanks to you, Penny."

"It's not just me. Harriet slaved for three days making those cookies and other people helped, too." Penny grinned at Jake.

"That's how it works. Even I feel good about playing you know who," he said, carefully making sure no one could hear them. "Those kids were great."

They both turned and looked at Hunter and Sally where they had been, greeting the little children.

"They won't run out of cookies, will they?" Jake suddenly asked.

"No, they shouldn't. We usually have plenty left over, and we made a few extra bags this year since the festival has been growing."

"Good. I'm even happy about helping with the cookies. Makes me feel a part of the community."

"So you should. You've helped a lot this year."

There was a gasp from most everyone around the tree and Jake and Penny looked up to see the white snowflakes falling from the sky.

"Santa is right on schedule this year, isn't he?" Penny asked with a big smile.

"Absolutely," Jake agreed. Then he leaned over and kissed Penny's lips, almost as if kissing her was a habit. Penny closed her eyes and melted into him. She didn't know how long it went on for, but when it was over she stared at him in surprise.

"Come on, let's get closer to the choir," Jake said, pulling her along behind him as if he hadn't just done something remarkable.

Penny supposed he'd been moved by the moment. His earlier kisses had been teasing, quick almost, but this kiss had been longer, more intense. Like everything else this evening, the kiss had felt just right. The snowflakes were certainly beautiful and appropriate. The weatherman hadn't mentioned any big storm tonight, so there was no big rush of people leaving to get home before the storm worsened.

They joined the crowd in front of the choir, perched on risers so they all could be seen. Proud parents were pointing out their children to their neighbors. Suddenly a floodlight was turned on a spot beside the choir and the audience could see a nativity scene, complete with a sheep, a donkey and a real baby.

"Hey, that's a real baby," Jake whispered.

"Yes, the choir director had him last summer. She volunteered him for the nativity scene. Believe me, he's wrapped warmly."

"He must've just had a bottle, too, because he's not complaining," Jake pointed out.

"I didn't know you knew that much about babies," Penny said with a chuckle.

"Everyone knows that much," Jake assured her.

As the snow began coming down a little thicker, Jake put his arm around Penny, drawing her against his big, warm body. For the first time in a long time she felt safe standing in his casual embrace. But as the thought lingered it was quickly replaced with a niggling doubt, because she didn't think it meant anything to Jake.

For their last song, the choir sang "Silent Night," and invited the crowd to join in. All their voices together created a magical moment next to the Christmas tree.

Then the crowd began breaking up.

"We need to find Harriet and see what we need to pack up," Jake said, finally breaking the magical mood. Penny turned back to the other side of the tree and together they went in search of Harriet.

In Jake's truck, the threesome set out for home. They had plenty of leftover cookies to eat on the way, though only Jake seemed to be eating them. Harriet and Penny were mesmerized by the snowflakes that drifted down from the sky.

"Aren't they beautiful?" Penny asked. "I've never seen such big flakes."

"I know. It's like God saved these just for tonight," Harriet said in agreement.

"Let's just hope they don't get thicker," Jake muttered.

"Are they making the drive difficult?" Penny asked.

"Not yet and I'm sure we'll be back to the

ranch before they get worse." After a moment, he asked, "Will there be enough packs of Santa cookies left for me to take for the men? I doubt they've ever gotten special cookies like those."

"Of course there are, Jake. I'll count out enough packs for you right now," Penny said. She was holding the Santa cookies on her lap.

"Just count seven packs, Penny. I've already had enough cookies tonight."

"I think we can spare another pack for you, too. After all, you did help make them."

"Okay, so maybe I'll eat just a few more."

Harriet and Penny laughed together.

"They go well with coffee," Penny said.

"That sounds like a good idea. Maybe Cookie has left a pot on the stove."

Penny paused slightly before she spoke next, not sure whether she should say what she was thinking. Eventually she decided to go for it. "You can always come to the house for a coffee if you'd like. I'm planning on a cup before I go to bed tonight. I want to be sure my toes are thawed out."

"I don't want to impose on you," Jake said.

"You won't be imposing. We can all share a pot and I think after the effort we all made for the Christmas festival we certainly deserve it," Penny insisted.

"Okay, you talked me into it."

Five minutes later, they pulled into the yard and Jake parked his truck close to the back door of the house. "Here, Penny, let me carry those boxes for you," Jake said.

Penny thanked him and they all rushed through the snowflakes to the back door. Harriet scooted in first and immediately began filling the coffeepot.

Penny and Jake came in after her. Penny began putting some logs in the kitchen fireplace and lit the kindling. She blew on the small flame until it caught the kindling, and there was soon a roaring fire.

Jake got down three mugs for the soon-to-be brewed coffee and set them on the table. Harriet added cream and sugar.

"I didn't know you took cream in your coffee, Harriet," Jake said.

"Just when I'm having some late at night. It helps me sleep," she said with a smile. "If you don't mind, I'm going to take my coffee to my room. I'm planning on going to bed."

"Sure, Harriet," Jake said. "Good night."

Penny got up from the fire now that it was burning well, and echoed Jake's words. Then she said, "Maybe I'll try cream tonight, although I doubt I'll need any help getting to sleep—I'm so tired."

Jake handed her a mug of coffee and took a sip of his own. "So, what's Hunter doing in town? Does he have a job?" Jake asked.

"I don't know. The only thing I know about him is that he played Santa for us tonight, like you did. I couldn't even recognize him if I saw him on the street."

"Me, neither. Unless he was dressed like Santa," Jake added with a grin.

Penny smiled. "He seemed nice, though, don't you think?"

"Maybe. You don't think Sally's interested in him, do you?" Jake asked.

"I don't know, Jake. There seemed to be something between them tonight, but it could have been something in the air, it was a magical night."

Penny opened several boxes. "I have oatmeal-raisin cookies and chocolate chip cookies. What do you prefer?"

They each took some of each kind of cookie and sat down for their late night coffee party.

"I think you can tell a lot by a person's name," Jake said. "Don't you?"

"Hmm, Hunter," Penny said. "I'm not sure what that says about him."

"It sounds like someone not from Bailey," Jake said.

Penny wore a worried frown. "It doesn't sound like a small town kind of name does it? But I hope he's planning on sticking around if Sally is interested in him."

"You're not her mother, Penny," Jake said softly.

"No, I know that, but I'm all she's got."

"Will your choice be vetted by your cousin?"

"Yes, I expect he will," Penny said. "At least I would hope Sally would be interested in looking out for me."

A silence fell between them and the thought of Penny's choice of husband made her feel a little uncomfortable sitting with Jake suddenly. Penny took a sip of her coffee, avoiding Jake's direct look, and nibbled a little at her cookie.

"Anyway," she said nervously, breaking the

silence. "I'm sure that kind of thing is a long way off."

Jake simply raised his mug to his lips and smiled.

The next day was Sunday.

Penny and Harriet had breakfast before they dressed, then they got ready for the drive to the small church in Bailey. Penny hoped to see Sally there. She was growing a little uneasy the more she thought about Hunter. He hadn't had a local accent, come to think of it and he'd sounded like he'd come from the Midwest, or maybe even farther east.

So what was he doing in Bailey?

Though the service was pleasant, Sally wasn't there. She and Harriet talked about going by the store, but it was locked up and there was no answer.

"There's nothing you can do about it now, Penny," Harriet assured her. "You can call her later on and ask her some questions then. I'm sure there's nothing to be concerned about, though."

"I guess so. But I can't help worrying about her."

As they pulled up beside the house, Harriet nodded in the direction of their back door.

"I think you're going to have something, or maybe I should say someone, taking up the rest of your afternoon. You won't have time to worry."

Penny looked in the direction Harriet was staring and saw Jake leaning against the wall next to the back door.

"What could he want?" she asked.

Harriet chuckled. "Who knows, but I'll bet you're going to find out real soon."

CHAPTER TEN

JAKE breathed a sigh of relief as he saw Penny's car pull up next to the house. He'd figured they'd arrive shortly, but he was getting a little cold. He straightened away from the wall and waited for them to reach him.

"Hi, Jake," Penny said, frowning slightly. "Is something wrong?"

"No, not at all. I just thought we should continue your shooting lessons today."

She looked surprised. "I don't think—"

"I do," he hurriedly said.

Before they could argue the matter, Harriet said, "It's time for lunch first, Jake. Come in and eat with us. Then you two can go shoot up some wood."

"I shouldn't—"

"You can't stand out here in the cold. Come on in."

"She's right, Jake. Let's eat lunch. Then we'll decide what to do."

Jake followed the two women into the house. The warmth of the house surrounded him and he shrugged off his coat and hung it on a hook by the back door. "What can I do to help, Harriet?"

"You can help Penny set the table."

Jake looked at Penny, who had carefully avoided looking at him. "Well, Penny?"

"I'm going to make a salad. You can set the table by yourself. The silverware is in that drawer."

Harriet gave Penny a sharp look. Then she looked at Jake. He shook his head. He couldn't explain Penny's mood. But he thought it must have something to do with her shooting lessons. He remembered they'd had a little difficulty last time because Jake had been determined not to touch her. But he had. That had forced him to take a step back, and it had obviously caused a little problem for Penny.

Now he didn't want to step away. He wanted to get closer to Penny. Much closer. But he thought he should take it slow. He didn't want to scare her.

He put the silverware on the table. By then Harriet had coffee made and poured him a cup. "Sit down, Jake. We can take it from here."

Jake did as Harriet said, taking a seat at the table, which made it possible to concentrate on Penny. She was still dressed for church in a slim dress that flared out below her hips. She didn't look anything like the determined rancher he'd seen those first few days. Last night at the Christmas Festival, she'd been enchanting.

Penny finished making the salad and brought it to the table, then she moved over to the cabinet where the glasses were stored. Soon she brought the iced tea to the table, setting a glass at each place.

Harriet brought over several more dishes and soon they were sitting down to lunch.

With little encouragement from either of the others, Harriet carried the conversation at the lunch table, discussing again the wonderfulness of the Christmas festival.

"It made me feel so good, last night, knowing that I'd helped so many people. I mean, I always try to help out where I can, but last night was special."

"Yes, it was," Penny agreed.

"Yeah," Jake agreed.

With that minimal encouragement, Harriet continued on, while the other two ate in silence.

When lunch was over, they assisted in the cleanup. Then Jake looked at Penny. "So, are you ready to try shooting lessons again?"

"I suppose so, but I'll have to go change my clothes first."

"All right. I'll go get the guns," Jake said.

After Jake had selected a rifle and a pistol, he sat down at the table to wait for Penny. Harriet was working at the counter, but she turned to look at Jake.

"You be careful with her, Jake. Okay?"

"Sure, Harriet. I'm going to make sure she knows exactly what she's doing with a gun."

"That's good. But I mean about other things, too."

"What are you talking about?"

"I mean, she's vulnerable right now. Her parents haven't been gone long and she's had a lot to deal with. She's had to fire the man she thought she trusted and hire you at a moment's notice. All those changes make it hard to get everything right."

Jake took a deep breath and released it slowly, looking thoughtfully at Harriet. "I'll go slow, Harriet. I want to get it right, too."

Harriet nodded and continued with her chores.

Penny came through the door. "I'm ready."

Jake thought she looked so cute, her cheeks flushed, standing there in jeans, sweater and a coat. It made it hard to remember what he'd just promised Harriet.

"Okay, I've chosen the rifle we used last time and a pistol. And I got the bullets we'll need. Let's go down behind the house and fire into that hill. That will stop the bullets from going anywhere we don't want them to go."

"Yes. Harriet, you know where we are if you need me?"

"You two be careful. I can come get you if I need to."

They moved outside and walked down to the place they were going to practice. Jake handed Penny the rifle and some bullets, watching carefully as she loaded the gun.

He knew she'd learned something from the

time before, since she carefully kept the rifle pointed down.

When she was ready, she asked about a target.

Jake walked down the hill and placed a piece of wood against a tree. Then he came back to Penny's side.

"Okay, hit the target."

She brought the rifle up and squared her shoulders, holding the gun tightly against her cheek. She lined up the sight with the target and squeezed the trigger.

"Hey! You hit it first time, Penny. That's great!"

She lowered the rifle, pointing it to the ground. "Thanks, Jake. It felt so much easier this time."

"Try to hit it a few more times."

After a fairly successful practice with the rifle, Jake brought out the pistol. "Now, this will be a little more difficult. Here are the bullets. Do you know how to load it?"

"No, I don't," Penny said, feeling slightly nervous.

He showed her the release on the barrel and how to insert the bullets. "Some people leave the chamber empty for safety, but this has a safety catch on it. You'll be fine as long as you keep it on. When you're shooting, you'll need to use both hands to hold it steady and line up the sight. Here, try it."

Penny's first shot missed the target entirely.

"Here, let me show you," Jake said and put his arms around her, placing his hands over hers. "Hold it steady and squeeze the trigger like you did with the rifle. Don't jerk the gun."

As Penny felt Jake's arms come around her she knew that her doubts had come true. She didn't want Jake to let her go…

Harriet heard the knock on the back door and guessed that one of the cowboys needed to talk to Jake. When she opened the door, she was quite surprised to see a young woman dressed more for a town outing than a ranch visit.

"Hello. May I help you?" Harriet asked.

"Yes, I hope you can. I'm Dexter Williams's wife. Penny paid a visit to the ranch while I was out and I thought I'd come visit her." The woman smiled, but Harriet wasn't too impressed. She knew that Penny hadn't been anywhere on her own in the last few days.

"I'm afraid her foreman is giving her shooting lessons right now. Can I take a message?"

About that time, they heard the shots.

"They sound close by. Do you know where they are?"

"Yes, back behind the house there's a low spot that is good for target practice." Harriet looked at her feet, clad in leather pumps. "But I'm not sure you've got the right kind of footwear for the walk."

"Oh, I'll manage. Thank you."

Before Harriet could say anything else, the woman turned and headed around the house.

Penny was trying to concentrate on shooting straight, but it was hard with Jake's arms around her. And he didn't draw away, this time.

With his help, she managed to hit the target.

"Do you see the difference between the pistol and the rifle?" Jake asked.

"Yes, but I'm not sure I've got the pistol down yet. We'd better try again."

Like magic, Jake's arms came around her again and she felt surrounded by safety and something a little more exciting.

"How…friendly," a cool, female voice said.

Both she and Jake tensed and the shot went astray. She brought down the pistol and looked behind her where a beautiful woman stood.

"Hello, Jake," the woman said.

"Penny, this is Angela Williams, Dexter's wife."

"Hello," Penny said, feeling less attractive in her jeans.

"Hello, Penny, dear," the woman said, her voice very condescending. "I'm sorry I haven't met you before. I hope you won't mind if I have a word with your foreman? We're old friends."

Penny realized that this was probably a woman Jake had been involved with before, and she stiffened, only giving a nod of her head in response.

Jake shot her an angry look, which she didn't understand, and walked over to Angela Williams.

"Jake, darling, I've missed you," Angela said softly reaching out to touch his chest.

He pushed her hand away. "What do you want, Angela?"

"What I've always wanted. You."

"I've told you I don't mess around with married women."

"I'd have come sooner," she whispered, as if

she hadn't heard his response, "if I'd known where you were, but Dexter wouldn't tell me."

"So how did you find out?"

"I had to go to the boring Christmas festival last night and I saw you with Little Mary Sunshine. I only had to ask a couple of people before they identified her."

"So?"

"Now that I know where to find you, we can continue. It will be much easier because we'll be away from Dexter's prying eyes."

"No, Angela, there's nothing to continue. I don't want to see you, in fact I don't want anything to do with you."

Her mood quickly changed from lover to enemy. "So! I guess you've found a better way to get your own spread." She was speaking louder now, obviously hoping their audience of one would hear. "You're courting the innocent female owner. You'll have your own place in no time, once you convince her to marry you. Very clever!"

Then she leaned forward and kissed Jake, taking him by surprise. "Good luck," she said and whirled around to walk back to her car.

Jake knew at once the damage Angela had

done, as she had intended. Penny's eyes were wide with shock. Then she picked up the rifle, already holding the pistol, and turned to walk back to the house.

"I don't want to practice anymore, Jake," Penny said and followed Angela's footprints around the house.

"Penny, wait! Let me explain."

She never stopped walking, her shoulders stiff with anger. She'd obviously believed everything Angela had said.

Harriet looked up as Penny came inside.

"Did your friend find you, Mrs. Williams I think her name was?"

"She's not my friend. She's Jake's friend." Penny kept on walking toward the den where her father had kept his guns.

Harriet followed her. "She said she came to see you because you called at her ranch when she was gone."

"No. She came to see Jake."

"Oh." After a moment, as Penny put the guns away, she asked, "Did I do wrong by telling her where you were?"

"No." Penny locked up the guns and turned

and headed up the stairs. "I'm going upstairs now, Harriet. I'll be down for supper."

Harriet followed her to the bottom of the stairs and watched as she hurried to her bedroom. Once inside Penny shut the door behind her. Then she cried the tears that she'd been holding in until she was alone.

She'd thought Jake was—was interested in her. He'd been so warm and friendly last night. And he'd put his arms around her while he was giving her shooting lessons, not drawing back as he had last time.

Dreams of she and Jake married, living on the ranch, carrying on the traditions her father and mother had begun, had filled her head. But she'd been foolish to be so easily conned. Angela had wiped those dreams away with her bitter accusation of Jake. Suddenly Penny had seen the obvious. It wasn't her who was enticing Jake. It was her ranch.

What was she going to do? How could she keep Jake as her manager when all he wanted was her ranch?

More tears followed as she wallowed in her misery. She wished she could talk to Sally, but she didn't want to admit her foolishness. She'd allowed herself to trust Jake and had thought that she could mix business with pleasure. Well, she would have to keep her mistakes to herself if she wanted to save face. She'd also make it perfectly clear to Jake that she knew what he was up to. He'd stop trying to charm her, then, wouldn't he?

She finally fell asleep on her bed, her arms wrapped tightly around her, as the events and feelings of today went round and round in her head.

The next morning, Penny dressed in her rancher gear, jeans, a sweater and a warm coat and hat, ready to go back to work learning about ranching.

When she got to the barn, ready to saddle Stormy to go out for the day, Jake stopped her.

"Penny, we need to talk."

"There's no time. I need to saddle Stormy."

"I think today's work is too dangerous for you. We're going to be separating yearlings from their mamas. You'd have to ride a cutting horse, and you're not experienced enough to—"

"I'm going out today, Jake. Get me a cutting horse if that's what I need, but I'm going out."

Jake stood there with his hands on his hips, staring at her. Finally he turned to Dusty. "Get Bulldog in and saddle him for Penny."

Dusty stared at Jake. "Bulldog?"

"That's right. She has to ride a cutter if she's going to participate today."

Dusty took a bridle and went out into the pasture to get the horse Jake had asked for. Bulldog was a black gelding, seemingly gentle. Penny stared at him as Dusty led him to the corral.

"He looks nice," she said tentatively.

"He's a cutter. The important thing to remember is to stay on his back. Hold on to the saddle horn if you have to, Penny. Cutters can be hard to ride if you're not prepared for the sudden movement."

"I'll manage," she said stiffly.

"Do you need some help mounting him?" Jake asked.

"No." She didn't think she could stand it if he touched her today.

When Dusty brought the horse to Penny, she swung into the saddle as if she knew exactly what she was doing.

They set out for the herd, the one closest to the house.

"Hang back, Penny. And remember, Bulldog is a cutting horse. He'll instinctively go for any cows that break away from the herd."

"I heard you the first time, Jake," Penny assured him, keeping her voice cool. He was treating her like a novice, but she'd been riding horses since she was a child.

The men began moving through the herd, separating the cows from the calves they'd had the previous spring. Most of the cows were carrying a new calf and having the older calf still nursing made life difficult for them. But they wouldn't willingly give up their calves.

The cowboys roped the yearlings and dragged them to a corral. Other cowboys kept the mama cows from attacking the cowboys. Penny had never seen this process before. She felt the pain of the mama cows, totally absorbed in what was happening.

When a yearling left the herd, with several of the cowboys in pursuit, they headed toward Penny. She was sitting relaxed in the saddle, having forgotten Jake's advice earlier.

Suddenly Bulldog was in pursuit, trying to stop the yearling. Penny reached for the saddle horn, having remembered Jake's warning, but she was too late. Suddenly she was flying through the air and landed with a thud, her head hitting a rock.

"Penny!" Jake called as he watched her fall from the saddle. He put his horse in a dead run to get to her side and ensure that she was okay. He felt guilty for letting her come with them today and not keeping more of a watchful eye on her, but he could tell she'd been too angry to accept his judgment.

When he reached her side, he pulled his horse to an abrupt stop and threw himself from the saddle. She wasn't moving and fear filled his heart. He knelt down beside her and saw her head resting against a rock. The other cowboys reached him a couple of minutes later.

"What happened to her, boss?"

Jake carefully turned her over, but she didn't open her eyes. "I think she hit her head against this rock when she fell. Dusty, go get one of the pickups and drive it out here as quick as you can. You'll take her to the doc in town. Maybe you should get Harriet to go with you."

"Don't you think you should be the one to—" Dusty began.

"No. She's angry with me right now. Go! Hurry! I want her to be checked by the doc as soon as possible."

Dusty didn't argue any more. He set off for the house at a run, determined to get Harriet first thing. He didn't know what Penny had been angry about, but he didn't want to face her by himself.

Jake sat there, cradling Penny in his arms, unable to think of anything else. He blamed himself for keeping his distance, hoping she'd forget her anger after a while. He should've insisted she listen to him.

But it wouldn't matter much now. Angela had made a pretty impressive show and he didn't think he could convince Penny that his interest in her was personal. The ranch didn't matter one bit if she wasn't part of the deal.

But how could he ever convince her?

In those dark moments, he finally accepted the truth. It would be best if he left Penny to get on with her life and find a new ranch manager. He'd find another job, far away from Bailey, Colorado.

CHAPTER ELEVEN

HARRIET hung on for dear life as Dusty drove the truck over the rough land, not bothering to go slow. Jake had told him to hurry, and that was what he was doing.

"Did she come to?" Harriet finally managed to ask.

"Not while I was there. Jake said to hurry."

Harriet had hurried when Dusty had reached the house, telling her that Penny had fallen from her horse and hit her head on a rock. She'd grabbed a pillow and a blanket, fearing Penny might be in shock.

Now Harriet was beginning to think *she* might be in shock by the time they reached Penny. Just when she was about to ask Dusty to slow down, he threw on the brakes, almost sending Harriet through the front windshield.

"We're here," he announced as he bailed out of the truck. Harriet managed to move quickly, too, though not as fast as Dusty.

"Jake, has she come to yet?" he asked.

Harriet could see that Penny's eyes were still closed. She hurriedly spread the blanket over her. "Can you carry her to the truck, Jake? I assume you're coming with us?"

"No, Harriet, I—I have to stay here. Dusty will take both of you to the doc."

Harriet stared at him. What was going on here? He was holding Penny like he'd never let her go, but he was choosing to stay with the cows instead of going with her to the doctor's? "Can't Dusty take your place here?"

"No. You'd better get back in the truck, and I'll hand Penny in to you."

Harriet did as Jake said, feeling there was something she wasn't understanding. She got in the front seat, the pillow in her lap and waited for Penny to be passed in. Jake lifted Penny over Harriet and put her head in Harriet's lap.

"Take good care of her," Jake whispered to Harriet. Then he backed away, his gaze remaining on them, waiting for Dusty to drive away.

Harriet pulled the door and nodded to Dusty. "Okay, we're ready."

"Shall I go as fast as we came?"

"You might take it a little easier. I'm not sure all that shaking would be good for Penny's head."

"Oh, right."

They hadn't gone very far before Penny opened her eyes. "What—where am I?"

"You're in the truck. We're taking you to see the doctor," Harriet explained. "Jake's orders."

Penny looked at the driver. "Dusty—where's Jake?"

Dusty cleared his throat. "He, uh, he had to stay there and handle—you know—what we were doing. I promised to get you to the doctor."

Penny swung her feet to the floorboard of the truck and sat up. For a brief moment, her head spun around, or at least that was what it felt like. Then she settled back in the seat. "I don't need to go to the doctor."

"Yes, you do, Penny," Harriet said firmly. "You hit your head on a rock."

"Because I forgot I was riding a cutting horse. It was my own fault. I'm perfectly all right now."

"I'll stop worrying about you when the

doctor tells us the same thing. Until then, we're taking you to see him."

Tears welled in Penny's eyes. "It doesn't matter anyway. Nothing matters anymore."

"What are you talking about, Penny?" Harriet demanded. "What doesn't matter?"

Dusty gave Penny a sideways look, reminding her that she and Harriet weren't alone. "Nothing. Never mind."

Penny stopped talking and so did the other two in the truck. They drove all the way into town without saying anything. When they got to the doctor's office, Penny slid out of the truck, almost falling against Harriet.

"Now, see, child, you need to see the doctor," Harriet said, wrapping an arm around Penny.

Inside, they only had to wait a couple of minutes before the doctor could see them. Harriet walked Penny into the examining room, leaving Dusty sitting in the waiting room.

The doctor asked Penny several questions and examined her. Then, as if Penny couldn't hear him, he suggested to Harriet that she keep Penny down for the rest of the day and see how she felt in the morning. "If she experiences any dizziness, make her stay in bed tomorrow also."

After they left the office and were once again in Dusty's truck, Penny railed against the doctor. "He's too cautious. I'm fine. I need to go back and watch them work the herd. I'm learning a lot, Harriet."

"Absolutely not! The doctor said you were to go to bed, and that's what you're going to do. It wouldn't hurt you to have a day off, anyway."

"I took Sunday off."

"No, you had some shooting lessons, I think. Come to think of it, that's when you started acting strange. Is there something you're not telling me?"

That question stopped Penny's complaints. She stared out the truck window the rest of the way to the ranch. Once there, she didn't argue about going upstairs to bed. In fact, she let Harriet tuck her in as her mother used to do when she was ill.

That behavior worried Harriet all the more. She came down to the kitchen to pour Dusty a cup of coffee, wearing a frown.

"What's wrong? Did she get dizzy?"

"No, Dusty, I don't know what's wrong. But she let me tuck her in bed, like she was a little child. I don't think she's acting like herself."

"You know, Jake hasn't been acting like himself, either, and it all started Sunday afternoon. At least that's what I think."

"Did they have an argument?"

"I didn't hear one."

"Me, neither…"

"What do I tell Jake?" Dusty asked.

"Tell him the doctor said she should be all right, but she is supposed to remain in bed the rest of the day and maybe tomorrow."

"Okay. Then I'd better get back out there and see if I can help with the work." Dusty said before he left the house.

Harriet poured herself a cup of coffee and sat down at the table, trying to figure out what was going on. She'd thought Jake was interested in Penny and Penny in him. She'd seen the signs before and they'd both shown hints in the past two weeks. But suddenly, something had happened and it had to do with that Williams woman.

Come to think of it, Penny had said the woman was there to see Jake, not her. Was she an old flame of Jake's? If so, Penny was ten times prettier in Harriet's eye.

With a sigh, Harriet got up to start making a

cake. She wanted to have something to tempt Penny's appetite. And maybe Jake's, too, if he came by to see how Penny was doing.

Dusty parked the truck in its usual place and re-saddled his horse to ride back out to where Jake and the other men were working the herd. When he reached them he waved to Jake and started helping Barney and one of the other cowboys with a yearling they were chasing. When he heard thundering hooves, he looked up to see Jake racing toward him.

"Dusty, what did the doctor say?" Jake demanded.

"Um, he said she should go to bed today and maybe tomorrow, depending on how she felt in the morning. He thinks she'll be just fine."

"When did she wake up?"

"Just after we left here. She said she didn't want to go to the doctor, but Harriet insisted."

Jake drew a deep breath. "It took you a long time to get back."

"I didn't want to run my horse any more than I had to. I raced all the way to the house to get the truck."

"Yeah, sure, I should've thought of that. Okay. Thanks, Dusty."

"Uh, boss, Penny wanted to know why you didn't go with them."

Jake stared at the cowboy and then looked out into the distance, seemingly lost in his thoughts. Finally he asked, "What did you say?"

"I said you needed to be here with the other cowboys."

"Good. Thanks."

Jake rode back to the other side of the herd, but his mind wasn't on the cows. It was on Penny. He was glad she'd had Harriet to help her, but he wished he had been the one she'd turned to. Everything had seemed so wonderful Saturday night. He'd even kissed her, a couple of times. They'd had their first kiss, and then their last kiss, on the same night, he thought mournfully.

He figured he could teach Dusty enough in a month for him to take over his duties temporarily. Then Jake would be free to leave. But he had nowhere he wanted to be except right here on Penny's ranch. He supposed he did have another choice, he could stay and be miserable for the rest of his life.

Why not? He was going to be miserable if

he left, so what difference did it make? But he remembered the look on Penny's face when she'd overheard Angela's words. If he stayed, he'd be making Penny miserable, too. He didn't want that.

When they finished work, after caring for their horses, the men all headed for the bunkhouse. Jake stood staring at the big house, wondering if he dared go ask about Penny. Probably it would just be Harriet in the kitchen. Penny would never know he'd even called.

He headed toward the house, his mind made up. He had a right to check on Penny's status. After all, he was still the ranch manager right now.

He knocked on the back door.

Harriet swung it open. "Jake. Come on in."

Jake stepped into the kitchen and realized he'd miscalculated. Penny was sitting at the table.

"Uh, hello, Penny. I didn't expect to see you up. How are you feeling?"

"Fine, thank you."

Her voice was cool, nonresponsive, in Jake's opinion. "No headache?"

She avoided his look. "I'm fine."

He turned to Harriet, but before he could ask her any questions, Penny said, "I hired you to manage the ranch, Jake, not me."

"Then please accept my apologies for disturbing you," he said stiffly and turned to the back door.

"Wait, Jake," Harriet pleaded. "I don't know what has upset the two of you, but surely you can work things out."

"No, Harriet," Jake said in a lower voice. "I'm not sure things can be as they once were, no matter how much we might want them to be." He looked at Penny seated at the table and noticed that she couldn't meet his gaze.

He left the house and walked slowly to the bunkhouse.

Yes, he definitely had to leave.

"Why are you so cold toward Jake, all of a sudden?" Harriet asked, sitting down at the table next to Penny.

"I don't know what you're talking about."

"Yes, you do. In the past we would've invited him to eat with us. You didn't even offer him a seat this time. There has to be a reason."

"Oh, Harriet, I can't—it was that woman, Mrs.

Williams. She's the one Jake was—was with in the past. And she accused him of flirting with me to—to get the ranch!" Tears filled her eyes.

"No! I don't believe it! Jake wouldn't do that!"

"Are you so sure? He—he's been flirting with me."

"Well, of course he has. You're a pretty young thing and you like him, too. Don't deny it. I've seen it in your behavior."

"Maybe I did, but I'm no fool! My father was fooled once by a man he trusted and I won't fall for the same thing. I won't be courted for the sake of my ranch!"

"I'm telling you Jake wouldn't do that! He's a good man. Hasn't he always been honest with you?" Harriet asked.

"Yes, but it's so obvious. I should've known better!"

"You're believing that woman, over Jake? Personally, Penny, I know which one I'd believe."

Penny looked at Harriet. "You really don't think that's what he's doing? Trying to get the ranch by marrying me? Think about it, though, Harriet, what would a man like Jake see in a woman like me."

Harriet smiled and put her arm around Penny. "Oh, honey, you still have so much to learn don't you. I'll be honest with you, I really don't think that Jake has any ulterior motives."

"Oh, Harriet, I don't know who to believe."

"Jake's only been here a few weeks, I know, but hasn't he always been honest with you, even if it's upset you? He didn't start flirting with you right away, did he? In fact, it seemed to me that he went out of his way to keep to himself. Now, would he have done that if his plan was to steal your ranch?"

Penny rubbed her temples.

"Is your head hurting?"

"Not as much as my heart is," she said softly, letting the tears escape her eyes to roll slowly down her cheeks.

Harriet gathered some tissues for Penny.

"Here, child, mop up. You've got to make the right decision. Jake may leave if you don't."

Penny buried her face in her hands. "I don't know what to do!"

Harriet patted her on her shoulder. "Just relax. You'll come up with something. I'll have supper ready in a minute."

She moved to the stove, throwing frequent

glances over at Penny, who had put her head down on her arms. Without her noticing Harriet moved to the telephone and picked it up. "Could you please ask Jake to come to the house when he finishes eating?"

After she hung up the phone, she sat back down beside Penny. "Jake is coming up here."

That awakened Penny from her stupor. "What? Why?"

"I asked him to come. It's time you two worked things out, starting tonight."

"No! No, I don't want to see him!" Penny jumped up from the table and ran up the stairs.

Just then there was a knock on the back door. Harriet got up and opened it to find Jake standing there.

"Come in, Jake."

"Hi, Harriet. Is everything all right with Penny?"

"She's fine. She's just taking a bath upstairs. She'll be down in just a minute. Sit down and I'll cut you a piece of cake.

"No, I'll come back later if she doesn't want—"

"Jake! Sit down. I think it's about time that me and you had a little chat."

Jake collapsed in a chair, burying his head in his hands, not unlike Penny's earlier response. "Yeah."

"Now, be honest with me Jake Larson. Are you courting Penny to get her ranch?"

"No! Of course not!"

"Then what is going on?"

"I—I've fallen in love with her. But Angela, Dexter's wife, said I was hoping to marry Penny so I could own my own ranch. It's because I don't want anything to do with her, I never have, but Angela thought she'd pay me back. Penny overheard her when we were shooting. But it's not true!"

"Of course it's not true!" Harriet agreed.

"I wish Penny was that easy to convince."

"What are we going to do about it?"

Jake released a breath, as though he'd thought long and hard about this question. "Well, the only thing I've figured out is for me to train Dusty to take over as manager and then leave."

"So then both of you would be miserable?"

"Harriet, I don't know anything else to do."

Harriet went to the fridge and cut a slice of cake, putting it in front of him. Then Harriet sat down at the table. "I don't either, Jake, but I think we should be able to come up with a better plan than that. We just need to think about it."

"I've thought and thought. No matter how much I swear that I just love her, the ranch will always be a part of the deal. And why would she accept a proposal from me when she believes such a terrible thing?"

"Have you proposed to her?"

"No, of course not! I mean, we've just started…I just thought she might…no. I'm not ready to propose yet. I've only kissed her a few times!"

"Well, the first thing you should do is kiss her a lot more times! No wonder she doesn't believe you're interested in her."

"I can't very well go around kissing her when she won't even talk to me."

"She'll talk to you about ranch things. I'll go and get her to come down to hear a report and then I'll leave you two alone—to talk."

"Harriet, I don't think—" Jake broke off as Harriet ran up the stairs. He sat there, not sure what to do. He wanted to see Penny, but he wasn't sure kissing her was the right approach.

It took several minutes before he heard a lighter step on the stairs. He held his breath, watching for Penny's entrance into the kitchen.

Suddenly she was there beside him. "Harriet said you had something to talk to me about—something to do with the ranch?"

"Yes. Would you like a piece of cake? It's very good."

"No, thank you."

"Well, at least sit down. I don't want you to get dizzy."

She sank into a chair, her eyes lowered.

"I wanted to tell you that, uh, we separated all the mamas from their babies. We'll go do the same thing for the other two herds tomorrow and the next day, for the same reason. Then we'll separate the yearlings by sex. We can keep the females to increase the herd, and sell the males when the market is at its highest, which should be around February."

"All right." She still kept her gaze on the table.

"Aren't you even going to look at me?" he asked suddenly.

Her eyes flashed up momentarily, then down again.

He decided to take Harriet's advice, even if it didn't make sense. He leaned over and kissed her, a soft, enticing kiss that he thought she responded to, at first. Then she jerked back. "Is that the end of your report?" she demanded in starchy tones.

"Uh, no, I…I think we should…count all the yearlings and then count each group separately, so we'll know how many we have to sell and how many additions to the heard we're going to make. You do want to increase the herd, don't you?"

"Yes, I think so."

He heard the indecision and decided another kiss would be important. Again, he leaned over and kissed her.

She pulled away again. "Jake, stop that!"

"You don't like to be kissed?"

"I don't want to be kissed just so you can get hold of my ranch!"

Jake looked seriously at Penny, but she couldn't meet his gaze. "Penny, do you trust and believe Angela more than you do me?"

Penny was silent for a moment before she answered. "What she said makes sense."

"No, it doesn't. Not if you know me, and I know you. Angela has nothing to do with us."

Jake reached over and took Penny's small hand in his own.

"I'm going upstairs now, Jake. I'm feeling a little dizzy all of a sudden. Will you excuse me?" She got up and walked out, but Jake was encouraged, just a little bit.

Harriet came back into the kitchen shortly after. "Well, did you talk to her?"

"I tried. And I took your advice, too. I kissed her, twice."

"How did she react?"

"Well, she protested both times, but I may have made a little progress. Thanks for the suggestion, Harriet, and thanks for being on my side," Jake said with a smile.

"Just remember, I'm on your side as long as you don't hurt her. If you hurt her, I'll be your worst enemy!"

CHAPTER TWELVE

PENNY stood at the window of her bedroom and watched Jake walk back to the bunkhouse. Harriet had made it clear that she believed Jake. But could Penny believe him? She had a lot more to lose than Harriet did.

But Jake had always been honest with her since his arrival. He'd told her the truth even when he knew she wouldn't like it. Why had he done that? If he did want to marry her just for her ranch, it didn't make any sense. When she'd told him to fire those three cowboys, he'd refused because he didn't have reason to fire them. If he'd wanted to please her, he'd have done as she said. Wouldn't he?

Holding her head in her hands, Penny wondered if she was losing her mind.

Then another question hit her. Why would

Dexter find a job for Jake if he believed he was
having an affair with his wife? Surely he would
have fired him? The only reason could be that
he didn't believe anything had been going on
between them and that what was happening
was not Jake's fault.

That was an interesting thought.

One she would consider overnight. She had
time to make her decision and thanks to Jake
she had a lot to think about.

She settled into her bed, trying to rethink
each argument and why she'd given it as much
credit as she had. In no time, she was again
confused. She desperately wanted to believe
Jake had meant all the things he'd said to her,
all the little touches or the few kisses, but she
had to have more time.

Tomorrow. Tomorrow she'd decide.

Penny didn't argue when Harriet said she
shouldn't ride out the next morning. She thought
a day in the house might be better for her.

After breakfast, Harriet started making
some cookies.

"Need any help?"

"I could use a little help. I've almost got

them mixed up. You can help put them on the cookie sheets."

"Why are you making more cookies?"

"I think they make a nice treat if you have a low moment in the afternoon. Or maybe someone drops in for a visit in the morning. You know, just something to serve people."

"That's nice, Harriet. But we're not expecting anyone, are we?"

"Not that I know of, but you never know. It's the holiday season, isn't it?"

"Yes, of course."

The two women worked together, finding it pleasant. When they'd finished Harriet suggested she make a grocery list for Penny.

"You can drive into town and have a nice shopping trip. It will give you something different to do."

"Yes, I'll be glad to get out of the house for a while."

"You're not feeling dizzy, are you?"

"No, I'm feeling fine, Harriet."

"All right. I'll see you in a little while."

Penny drove to town, enjoying the trip. It was so completely different from riding out on the ranch. Penny bought everything on

Harriet's list and got it all to the car. She thought about visiting Sally, but then decided against it. She didn't want to face her cousin when she was still so confused. Just as she was about to drive away, she saw someone she knew. Angela Williams was strolling down the street as if she didn't have a care in the world. She obviously didn't work.

"Well, if it isn't Little Mary Sunshine," Angela said with a nasty smile.

"No, it's Penny Bradford, Mrs. Williams. I don't think we were properly introduced the other day."

"Oh, I think we were. I know exactly who you are. Jake's leading you down the garden path, isn't he?"

"I don't think so. He's acting as my manager, and doing a very good job of it, too. Thank your husband by the way for recommending him."

Angela gave a sharp laugh. "He wanted to get him away from me! But he didn't send him far enough did he?"

"Oh? You mean Jake's been over to the ranch to see you?"

"No, he—yes, as a matter of fact he's been

over to see me several times," Angela said, changing her mind in midstream.

At that moment Penny knew she was lying. She could account for Jake's time almost entirely since he'd come to work for her. It was suddenly as if a cloud had lifted and she wanted nothing more than to get away from this woman. "I see."

"Yes. We're in love, you see. He begged me to leave Dexter."

"Oh? I'm surprised that you didn't if you and Jake are so in love."

"Well, I'm just not cut out to be poor you see. I need beautiful things around me."

"That's too bad," Penny answered, shaking her head in disbelief at the woman in front of her. "If you'll excuse me, Mrs. Williams, I have to go now. It's so nice to see you again," Penny lied.

"Call me Angela, won't you?"

"No, I don't think so, Mrs. Williams," Penny said, closing the door on her car and backing out of the parking space. As she drove home, she wondered if she'd made a mistake. She didn't want to offend Dexter after he had referred Jake to her, he had been a good friend of her father's after all. But she didn't want to appear friendly to that woman.

When she reached home, she didn't say anything about her encounter with Angela to Harriet. Instead she helped her put away all the groceries, smiling and chatting as if everything was normal.

Harriet watched Penny as she moved around the kitchen. She couldn't quite determine what had happened to change Penny's attitude, but something had certainly done the trick.

When dinner was ready, they were about to sit down and eat when a knock came on the door. Penny didn't move. Harriet, after looking at Penny, got up to answer the door. She found Jake standing there.

"Come in, Jake."

"I just wanted to report to Penny, is she here?"

"She's here. Are you going to join us for dinner?"

Jake looked at Harriet, unsure how to answer.

"You are very welcome to join us, Jake, if you'd like to, of course," Penny calmly responded.

Jake entered and Harriet hurried to set a place for him. "Did you have a good day, Jake?" Penny asked politely.

"Yes, we did. We separated out the yearlings from the second herd."

"You can tell me about it after dinner," Penny said. "I'd like to enjoy dinner tonight without worrying about any work details. Would that be okay with you?"

"Uh, sure, Penny, whatever you want."

After they were all served, Penny said, "I went grocery shopping for Harriet this afternoon."

"That's nice. You didn't feel dizzy, did you?"

"No, Jake, I didn't get dizzy. But I did meet a friend of yours."

"Oh, who's that?"

"Angela Williams."

Jake stopped eating immediately and looked Penny straight in the eyes. "She's no friend of mine."

Penny smiled at him, pleased at his passionate response. Jake returned to eating his dinner, but it was clear that he was not happy with the way the conversation was heading. Penny continued, "Angela was mentioning all the visits you've paid her since you started working here."

Again, Jake stopped eating and stared at Penny. "That's a damned lie! She didn't even know where I was until the night of the Christmas festival!"

Penny smiled. She'd thought that, but she hadn't been sure. Now she was. "It's okay, Jake. I know you're right."

"You do?" Jake asked, confused.

"Yes, I do. She lied to me."

"Yeah, she did."

"So maybe she was lying about the other thing, too."

Penny took a bite of potatoes and chewed deliberately.

Jake, keeping his gaze on Penny, also ate something. He had no idea what he'd put in his mouth, until he tasted the roast beef.

Harriet was watching both of them, afraid she would miss something. But there wasn't any more conversation during dinner.

Afterward, both Jake and Penny helped Harriet clean the kitchen. Then, with cups of coffee and a plate of cookies between them, Jake and Penny sat down to discuss ranch business. Harriet excused herself after making sure they had whatever they needed.

"So, tell me about your day," Penny said.

"We chased a lot of calves determined to outrun us."

"It sounds challenging."

"Yeah, it was," Jake said, and unable to resist any longer he leaned over to kiss Penny.

"I don't think you should do that," Penny said, a little flustered when he finally sat back.

"Why not?"

"B-because I'm not sure—"

"About what? You know Angela lied, don't you?"

"Yes, I know that."

"Well, then?"

"I thought you didn't want any flirting. I thought we had to keep things strictly business?"

"I've changed my mind." Jake smiled, his perfect white teeth stark against his dark, rugged skin.

"Why?" Penny asked, watching Jake closely, butterflies doing somersaults in her stomach.

"Because I've found I'm attracted to a young lady who is being strong in a difficult situation," he said, smiling again at Penny.

Penny blushed, ducking her head to avoid Jake's gaze. "I—I'm trying to do the right thing, Jake, but this is all very new to me. Maybe we should wait a little while to—to act on what we've been feeling."

"I'm glad you said we. I was beginning to think it was just me."

Penny forced herself to look at Jake. "No, it's not just you, but—but I haven't known you very long, and—"

He leaned over and kissed her again. Each kiss was growing longer and longer. When he finally pulled back, he said, "Okay, I understand. We'll take things slowly, but I'll see you tomorrow morning? You'll ride out with us again won't you?"

"Yes, I want to ride out with you."

He stood. "Then I'll see you in the morning. Good night, Penny."

"Good night, Jake."

After he left, Penny slowly went upstairs, Jake on her mind.

After two days recuperating, Penny was ready to ride out the next morning. Harriet fixed her a lunch to take with her.

Bundled up for the cold weather, Penny hurried to the barn, afraid she was a little late. But she found the corral full of riders, not having left yet.

Jake came to meet her as she entered the corral. "Good morning, Penny. I've got a nice horse ready for you. It's a filly named Red."

"That's not a very pretty name for a filly," she complained.

"Maybe not, but she's a safe ride. She's over here." He led Penny to the other side of the corral. "She's a cutter, too, but she's not as fast as Bulldog. She doesn't leap at an opportunity to get into the action. She'll be better for you."

Penny frowned at Jake. "You mean she's safe and slow."

"Exactly," Jake said with a smile.

"I think I'd rather have Bulldog."

"Not today. Maybe later when you're better equipped to handle him," Jake said and the concern was still evident in his voice.

With a grimace, Penny swung into the saddle, reaching forward to pet her horse. "I guess she'll do."

Jake swung into Apache's saddle. "Ready to go, men?"

"And lady," Dusty called out with a grin.

"Yeah, and lady." Jake led them out of the corral toward the herd they were working with today.

Jake pulled his horse aside until Penny rode next to him. Then he fell into line beside her. "I've found a job for you to do. It's not as exciting, but it's necessary."

"What job?"

"You can be the gate man."

"What does that mean?"

"Well, we're rigging up a temporary corral for the yearlings we separate from their mamas. You'll let the yearlings in and none of the cows."

"You're right. That doesn't sound very exciting."

"Too bad we're not alone right now," he murmured softly, watching her lips.

"Why?" she asked.

"Because I'm very tempted to kiss you."

"Jake! Not in front of the men!"

Jake grinned. "Once we're engaged, they'll expect that kind of behavior."

"I haven't...we're not...I'm going to go talk to Dusty."

She rode ahead and left Jake smiling mischievously behind her.

Penny asked Dusty about the corral they would put up.

"Didn't Jake tell you? It's a rope corral. We stick holders in the ground and attach a couple of ropes to it. The calves don't know how to get out. Logic isn't their biggest asset."

"Are you saying they're dumb?" Penny asked.

"Not dumb, exactly, but they don't understand. They think they have to stay inside the rope."

"Jake says I have to be the gate person. Is that going to be hard?"

"No, it's a nice safe job, boss. Jake wouldn't put you in danger, Penny. I thought he was going to have a heart attack when you fell off your horse."

"But he didn't go with me to the doctor, did he?"

"No. I don't know why. But I know he wanted to. He sure was worried about you when I got back from town. Couldn't stop asking me questions."

"Thanks, Dusty, for telling me that."

"Sure, Penny. Anytime."

Penny rode on silently the rest of the way until they reached the herd. She watched the men string up the rope corral, thinking being the gate person was definitely the easiest job there. However, Jake came over to talk to her.

"So you see what you have to do?"

"Yes, but wouldn't it be easier if I was on foot, rather than on a horse?"

"No! Absolutely not! That would make it hard for you to get out of the way of a calf that was acting up. On horseback, you'll be safe."

"Okay. You're the boss," she said slowly, still thinking about what he'd said.

After the corral was in place, she took the rope gate in her right hand, holding the reins of her horse in her left. "I'm ready."

"Okay, we'll get busy finding your first customer." Then he rode toward the herd. "Let's go, men."

It didn't take long for Penny to see why she was on horseback. Some of the calves were determined not to go in the rope corral. They had to be dragged through the gate and the lasso not taken off of them until they were in the corral with the gate shut. Then Penny had to open the gate for the cowboy or cowboys to ride out.

Each time a new calf was brought in, the other calves pressed against the back side of the corral. If they could just think, the calves would have a chance to escape, but they were dumb!

When it was lunchtime, Penny was surprised when all the men dismounted and got out a lunch. "I didn't know Cookie fixed you lunches," she said to Barney.

"It was Jake's suggestion. He said he had had a lunch or two with you, and it gave him more strength to finish the work. He suggested we all bring some lunch with us."

"I think that's very smart."

"What is smart?" Jake asked as he came over to Penny.

"You suggesting that the cowboys bring some kind of lunch."

"Yeah, well, I enjoyed the breaks we had when we were riding out together. And Harriet gave us some of the cookies she made the other day so it seemed a shame to waste them. Did you get some in your lunch?"

Penny pulled her sandwich out and discovered cookies wrapped up beneath the sandwich and apple. "Yes, she put some in my lunch, too."

"Good. Let's all enjoy our lunch," he said to

the others. "I meant to tell you I don't think I'll look for cowboys to replace the three who left. They apparently weren't doing much of the work. In the spring when we're ready for calving season, I'll try to hire a couple of new ones, but with me, that would make ten. That should be more than enough."

"You're saying Gerald didn't do much of the work, either?"

"I'm just saying I think we'll be comfortable with two more for the spring and summer."

Penny turned to face the other men. "Is that true? Didn't Gerald or the other three do much work?"

Dusty spoke up from around the circle. "Not really. We didn't understand why, but whatever they were assigned to do didn't get done."

"Why didn't you complain?"

"I did once to Gerald. He told me to mind my own business."

"Dad didn't know that. I promise he didn't think he was running that kind of operation."

"Your dad would've liked Jake," Barney said. "I think he was beginning to catch on to Gerald. I heard an argument between the two of them a few days before his death."

"What did they argue about?"

Barney shook his head. "Just arguing about why a job was taking so long. It was one those three no-good cowboys were supposed to be doing."

"Well, I don't run that kind of operation. If there's a problem, I want to know about it." Penny looked at all the men sitting in a group. They all smiled at her and Jake was beginning to worry that there might be more than one man falling in love with Penny.

"Okay, everyone, eat your lunches, before I make you go back to work early," Jake said with a smile.

By the time they'd finished the herd, Penny was exhausted. Then they had to drive the calves away from the herd to another pasture. That was the hardest part of all. Several calves broke free and had to be roped again and pulled with the herd. Once they got a fence between the two herds, life was easier. But they moved them several fences away.

It was approaching dark when they reached the barn. Penny almost fell from the saddle. Jake was beside her almost at once. "Go on to the house. I'll unsaddle your horse for you."

"No. I need to do it myself. Everyone did more work than me today. I shouldn't be babied just because I'm a girl."

"It's okay, Penny. You'll get stronger the more you do this. But for tonight, I want you to go to the house. You helped us today. We wouldn't have gotten finished without you doing the gate. So go on to the house."

"Will you come have dinner with us?" She'd made up her mind about Jake before she set out this morning, but she hoped for some privacy to tell him.

"Yeah, I'd like that. I'll be up in a few minutes."

"All right. Good night, everyone," Penny called as she headed for the house. Her legs were wobbly, but she got there. When she went in, Harriet was hovering by the stove.

"I didn't think you were going to make it. It's almost dark out there."

"I know, Harriet. I'm going to go take a quick shower before Jake gets here. I invited him to dine with us."

"Oh, good. I'll start warming things up."

Penny dragged herself up the stairs until she reached her room. Then she fell across the bed, exhausted. She didn't move for several minutes. The thought of Jake getting there and not finding her at the table forced her to undress and get in the shower. She lingered under the hot water because it took away the soreness.

Once she got out of the shower, she hurriedly dressed again and came down the stairs. But Jake had already arrived.

He looked at her as she came into the kitchen. "Are you all right? You worked hard today."

"Yes, I'm sorry. I stayed too long in the shower. You got a shower?"

"Yeah, I grabbed a quick one. I didn't want to smell like horses."

She smiled but didn't say anything. Sitting in her chair, she looked at Harriet. "Did we keep you waiting?"

"No, it's all ready. I just need to get the rolls. I didn't put them in until I heard you on the stairs."

Soon dinner was served and they all ate well. Penny felt like a bottomless pit, not sure she'd ever get full.

When the phone rang, Harriet got up and answered it. After a minute, she said, "Just a minute."

She motioned for Penny to come to the phone. Penny picked up the receiver. "Hello?"

"Penny, it's Dexter Williams. I'm sorry to call you but I don't have the bunkhouse number to reach Jake."

"That's not a problem, Mr. Williams. He's right here. Just a minute."

She motioned to Jake and he came to the phone.

Penny sat down. She wondered why Dexter Williams would be calling after Jake at this time of night, but she guessed it was none of her business. Whatever he needed Jake for it sounded as though it might be urgent.

"No, sir. I haven't seen her. No, the one time she came here, I told her I didn't believe in messing around with married women.

"Yes, sir, I know. I'll tell her if I see her, but I don't expect to. Yes, sir."

Then Jake hung up the phone.

Penny and Harriet said nothing.

Jake sat down and picked up his fork. He looked at Harriet and finally turned to face Penny before he spoke.

"It appears his wife has run away. He wanted to make sure she hadn't run away to me."

"He believed that she might?" Penny asked, a sharp pain suddenly shooting in her chest.

"He didn't think so, but he's desperate. He can't figure out where she's gone. I would guess she's found a new playmate…or a new place to run to. She'll probably come back soon, and he'll forgive her."

"How sad," Penny said, looking distressed.

"Penny, it's what she does. He chose that way of life when he chose Angela. They go hand in hand."

"That's not the kind of marriage my parents had," Penny said. "They loved to be together."

"That's the kind of marriage I want, too. One where I spend all the time I can with my wife."

"And children?" Penny asked.

"Of course I want children. How many do you want?"

"I think a dozen," she said calmly, continuing to eat.

Jake broke into congested coughing. After a moment, he said, "Did you say a dozen?"

"Yes, but I might settle for four."

"Four sounds a lot more reasonable."

Harriet said, "Four is a good number.

Between you and me, Penny, I think we could manage four."

"That's what I thought," Penny agreed.

Harriet smiled.

"Would my wife still be able to ride out with me on occasion if she had four kids?" Jake asked.

"Oh, I think so. With Harriet at home, I think I could ride out with my husband."

"Every day?"

"No, not every day. But when I could help out, like I did today, then I think I could manage."

"We are talking about the same marriage, aren't we?"

"We're just talking about a possibility," Penny said with a smile.

"When do we talk about it as a probability?" Jake asked.

Harriet stood and looked at both of them fondly. "If you don't mind, I think I might call it an early night. It's been a tough day."

When Harriet bid them good-night, Penny turned to face Jake. Her insides were suddenly all atwitter with excitement. She'd known for a while now that Jake was the man for her. She'd known he drew her as no one ever had.

But today's ride had confirmed what she'd thought. He'd been generous and strong with the other men and they clearly trusted him completely, unlike Gerald.

Jake Larson was a man's man, and most definitely a woman's man. Her man. She was sure he was the one for her. He would run the ranch well, and he would keep her happy. And he'd be a good father to her children, all four of them.

Jake was staring at her. "Are you sure, Penny?"

"Oh, yes, I'm sure," she answered, returning his gaze.

With his gaze on Penny, Jake stood and held out his hand to Penny. She stood, put her small hand into Jake's and walked to the den, Jake following behind her.

"Well, Penny, now that we are alone, will you marry me?"

"Why, Mr. Larson, I'm so shocked!"

Jake gathered her into his arms. "So am I, Penny. I thought you would make me wait until spring, at least."

She slid her arms around his neck. "No, I don't think I can wait that long."

He kissed her, a deep, satisfying kiss that made her think of marrying him sooner rather than later.

"Oh, Jake," Penny said with a sigh when his lips left hers. "I really like the way you kiss."

"I'm glad to hear it. You weren't responding much when I kissed you before."

"I had to be sure you were the one for me. But now I'm sure."

"Good. Kiss me again," he whispered, meeting her lips with his.

Half an hour later, Jake suggested they make a pot of coffee. Penny stared at him. "You don't like kissing me?"

"I like it fine, but it makes me want to do other things, and I think you'll want to wait until we're married. Right?"

"Yes, I guess so," Penny said and sat back away from Jake.

"Honey, say the word and I'll haul you up the stairs and we can make love all night long. But I'm prepared to wait if that's what you want."

With a sigh, Penny said, "It's what I want. Mom and I talked about my wedding, in the future, you understand. She talked about how special it was. Or could be."

He put his arm around her again and pulled her close. "Yeah. I want our daughters to wait, too."

She chuckled. "What if we have all boys?"

Jake kissed her. "I'll take whatever we get. The most important thing to me is marrying you and I want your wedding night to be special for you."

"So when should we get married?"

"As soon as possible."

"I don't want to tell Sally until Christmas Day. That will be a nice way to surprise her, especially after the year we have both had."

"That's a lovely idea. But if we tell her then, when will we be able to get married?"

"New Year's Day?"

"I like that. I want to start off the year with you as my wife."

"I think Mom and Dad would like that." She felt that amazing warm feeling she'd felt by the Christmas tree as if her mother was saying yes.

"I hope so. I feel like I know your dad, after reading his journals. I know he was an honest, good man."

"Yes, he was. Mom was the same kind of person."

"Well, together, we'll forge the same kind

of marriage they had. We'll just have a few more kids."

Penny put her arms around his neck again. "I like that, Jake. I like it very much." And she gave him another soul-shattering kiss.

MILLS & BOON
Romance

On sale 7th December 2007

*In a month filled with Christmas sparkle we bring
you tycoons and bosses, loves lost and found, and
little miracles that change lives...*

SNOWBOUND WITH MR RIGHT *by Judy Christenberry*

City slicker Hunter doesn't fit into Sally's world, but she's
beginning to wonder if she's snowbound with Mr Right!
The second **Mistletoe & Marriage** story.

THE MILLIONAIRE TYCOON'S ENGLISH ROSE
by Lucy Gordon

Freedom is especially precious to Celia. The last of the
Rinucci Brothers, Francesco, wants to wrap her in cotton
wool but hasn't bargained on her feisty spirit.

THE BOSS'S LITTLE MIRACLE *by Barbara McMahon*

Anna is poised for promotion when in walks new CEO
Tanner – the man who broke her heart a few weeks ago!
Then Anna discovers a little miracle has happened...

HIS CHRISTMAS ANGEL *by Michelle Douglas*

Do you remember *that* guy? The one from your past that
you never seem to be able to get over? Join Cassie as gorgeous
boy-next-door Sol comes home for Christmas!

MILLS & BOON

MEDICAL™

Proudly presents

Brides of Penhally Bay

A pulse-raising collection of emotional, tempting romances and heart-warming stories by bestselling Mills & Boon Medical™ authors.

January 2008
The Italian's New-Year Marriage Wish
by Sarah Morgan

Enjoy some much-needed winter warmth with gorgeous Italian doctor Marcus Avanti.

February 2008
The Doctor's Bride By Sunrise
by Josie Metcalfe

Then join Adam and Maggie on a 24-hour rescue mission where romance begins to blossom as the sun starts to set.

March 2008
The Surgeon's Fatherhood Surprise
by Jennifer Taylor

Single dad Jack Tremayne finds a mother for his little boy – and a bride for himself.

Let us whisk you away to an idyllic Cornish town – a place where hearts are made whole

COLLECT ALL 12 BOOKS!

FREE

4 BOOKS AND A SURPRISE GIFT!

We would like to take this opportunity to thank you for reading this Mills & Boon® book by offering you the chance to take FOUR more specially selected titles from the Romance series absolutely FREE! We're also making this offer to introduce you to the benefits of the Mills & Boon® Reader Service™—

- ★ **FREE home delivery**
- ★ **FREE gifts and competitions**
- ★ **FREE monthly Newsletter**
- ★ **Books available before they're in the shops**
- ★ **Exclusive Reader Service offers**

Accepting these FREE books and gift places you under no obligation to buy; you may cancel at any time, even after receiving your free shipment. Simply complete your details below and return the entire page to the address below. You don't even need a stamp!

YES! Please send me 4 free Romance books and a surprise gift. I understand that unless you hear from me, I will receive 6 superb new titles every month for just £2.89 each, postage and packing free. I am under no obligation to purchase any books and may cancel my subscription at any time. The free books and gift will be mine to keep in any case.

N7ZEE

Ms/Mrs/Miss/Mr...Initials ....
BLOCK CAPITALS PLEASE

Surname ....

Address ....

....

....Postcode ....

Send this whole page to:

The Reader Service, FREEPOST CN81, Croydon, CR9 3WZ